DANGER COVE

www.dangercovemysteries.com

DANGER COVE BOOKS

Secret of the Painted Lady
Murder and Mai Tais
Death by Scones
Four-Patch of Trouble
Deadly Dye and a Soy Chai
Killer Closet Case
Tree of Life and Death
A Killing in the Market (short story)
Killer Colada

BOOKS BY SIBEL HODGE

Danger Cove Cocktail Mysteries
Murder and Mai Tais
Killer Colada

Amber Fox Mysteries:
Fashion, Lies, and Murder
Money, Lies, and Murder
Voodoo, Lies, and Murder

Other Works:
Fourteen Days Later
My Perfect Wedding
The Baby Trap
How to Dump Your Boyfriend in the Men's Room (and other
short stories)
It's a Catastrophe
The See-Through Leopard
Trafficked: The Diary of a Sex Slave

Non Fiction:
A Gluten Free Taste of Turkey
A Gluten Free Soup Opera
Healing Meditations for Surviving Grief and Loss

KILLER COLADA

a Danger Cove Cocktail mystery

Sibel Hodge &
Elizabeth Ashby

KILLER COLADA

CHAPTER ONE

———

They say that death, divorce, and moving are right up there as three of the most stressful things in life, and in the last two months I'd been through everything but the divorce. It was awful enough when my boss and good friend, Bob, had been murdered, and when I found the second body, I was starting to think I could be some kind of death magnet. *But I guess I need to back up a bit.*

Bob owned and ran the Smugglers' Tavern in the quaint coastal town of Danger Cove, not far from Seattle, Washington. I'd worked for him as a bartender since I'd moved here a year ago, and we'd grown close. He hadn't been just my boss. He'd been more like a father figure, and evidently he'd felt the same way, because shortly before being murdered, he'd changed his will to leave his vast fortune, including the tavern, numerous rental properties in town, and a huge portfolio of stocks, gold, and savings, to me. You might think that sounded like a good thing, but unfortunately his scheming, gold-digging daughter, Elise, and lazy good-for-nothing nephew, Carter, didn't agree. Neither did the police. For a long time I was labeled as some kind of black widow who'd set out to entrap Bob into leaving me his fortune, and I'd been one step away from being locked up.

Fast-forward two months, and things were starting to brighten up a little. Although I still missed Bob, I was really grateful to have had him in my life, and I was convinced that he was still a presence hanging around me in the form of a three-legged kitten I'd named Karma, who'd padded into my life, more specifically my house, shortly after Bob's passing. Both Elise and Carter had now dropped their lawsuit to contest Bob's will and had slinked out of town to find some other rocks to crawl under, so my legal headache had gone away. And I'd moved out of the tiny but cute cottage I'd rented off Bob when I'd first moved into town and was now living in the spacious and rustic apartment above the tavern, which had amazing views of the Pacific Ocean, from the cliffs in front of the building, all the way past the old lighthouse, the harbor, and Two Mile Beach. And then there was Harvey Wynters, a British underwater archaeologist who'd arrived in town searching for the long-lost *Ocean's Revenge*, a smuggling ship that had disappeared in 1852, reported to have sunk somewhere off the coast. I'd had a strict no-dating rule for years after I'd caught my fiancé, Nick, cheating on me, but Harvey had saved my life when I'd ousted Bob's murderer, and the whole lifesaving thing kind of trumped the no-dating rule.

So, life had been messy for a while, but I guess it always was, and I was a big believer that everything happened for a reason. There would always be ups and downs, storms and lulls. There I was thinking I'd hit a lull, when another storm whipped up.

I was outside in the tavern's garden area, marking up the chalkboard with today's special cocktail, a Smugglers' colada laced with plenty of white rum, when Ruby walked up, her long red hair shimmering over one shoulder like a Danger Cove sunset. Actually, that was probably incorrect. Ruby didn't just walk. She flowed or bounced. Although she was in her late fifties, she exuded youth and vitality and was filled with more energy than anyone I'd ever met. She was an international yoga guru with her own renowned studio in Seattle, a huge following, and a string of DVDs under her belt. These days she spent less time teaching and more time running intimate yoga retreats in exotic places all over the globe. She'd also been helping me out in the tavern as a bartender and waitress because Bob's death had thrown everything into chaos. Carter and Elise used to work in the tavern, although that usually involved nail filing and flirting with the customers for Elise, and sleeping on the job for Carter. Now that they were both out of the tavern and out of my life, I was shorthanded until I could find some replacement staff. In fact, the tavern had also undergone an upheaval in the kitchen department. The previous long-standing chef, Charlie, was now history, and his kitchen assistant, Tara, had taken over. She was an excellent cook in her own right, who loved singing very loudly and very off key as she whipped up her gourmet creations. Her twin sister, Clara, was now her assistant, and they worked well together.

Like I said, things had been messy, but now I had a feeling the Universe's happy plan for me was unfolding.

"Hello, darling!" Ruby kissed me on both cheeks, continental style, before giving me a hug.

I hugged back. Ruby was the closest thing I had to a mom, and even though she wasn't the real thing, I loved her like one. My own parents had been alcoholics who'd lived in a commune. My dad died when I was seven, and my mom forgot I existed. I stuck it out until I was eighteen, then disappeared to travel the world, searching for the sense of family and belonging I'd been missing all those years. I finally found it in Danger Cove.

I breathed in Ruby's jasmine essential oil. "Morning. How are you?"

"I'm great." She rested her hands on my shoulders and looked deep into my eyes. She'd been worried about me since all this crazy stuff with Bob had happened. "But how are you?" With her fingertip, she swept away a tendril of my long waves that had blown messily across my face in the breeze. "I know you've been through a lot of upheaval lately."

I smiled. "No, I'm good. I'm getting there."

She linked an arm through mine and walked us back into the rustic interior of the tavern. I took a breath, inhaling the scent of the old oak floor and paneling around the bar, the salty air that always seemed to permeate the stone walls. I loved this place. And now it was all mine.

"Well, I had an idea that might de-stress you after the last few months." Ruby raised a knowing eyebrow. "I thought you could do with some spiritual therapy, so I've booked us both in for a crystal healing session this afternoon. We need to unblock your stagnant chakras and get some fertile energy flowing."

At that moment Vernon, who'd also been helping me out in the tavern, returned from collecting empty glasses and snorted loudly at Ruby. "Fertile okra? Crystal healing? What are you twittering on about now?"

"*Chakras*, not *okra*," Ruby said proudly.

Vernon shook his head with disbelief. "Sometimes I don't think we talk the same language."

"Yes, that had crossed my mind on more than one occasion."

Vernon and Ruby had history together. I hadn't known just how much until we'd investigated Bob's death. On the surface they were friends who bickered like an old married couple, but both of them were too stubborn and set in their ways to admit they still loved each other. Everyone in town thought Vernon was a retired teacher, a harmless good-natured old guy who liked a drink. Ruby and I were the only ones who knew that Vernon was actually an ex-FBI agent who'd retired to Danger Cove to be closer to Ruby, even though he'd never admit that out loud.

"When are you going for your crystal meth session?" Vernon put the glasses in the dishwasher.

"Just because you don't believe in all this doesn't mean it doesn't work. And Hope's been through a rough time lately. She needs a bit of positive energy to lift her spirits."

"It's all a load of mumbo jumbo."

"Yes, well—"

"Okay, guys," I interrupted before they could get into another round of sparring. "No more bickering today. Honestly, sometimes you guys give me a headache!"

Ruby opened her mouth to say something else to Vernon and then thought better of it. She turned to me. "I've booked us in at four so we can get back here before the dinner rush starts. How does that sound?"

I glanced at the clock—3:20 p.m. Then I cast a worried look at Vernon. The tavern was now my responsibility, and I was taking it seriously. I was a business owner now, and I wanted to do Bob proud and carry on his dream of running a friendly, local pub with excellent food and welcoming staff. I couldn't go traipsing off all the time and leaving people in the lurch. Especially when they were friends who were good enough to be helping me out. "Will you be all right here on your own until we get back?" I bit my lip.

Before Vernon could say anything, Ruby answered for him. "Of course he will. He's taken down hardened mobsters and gangsters. I think he can look after a bar for a few hours, can't you?" She tilted her head in a challenge.

He looked at me, and his gaze softened with sympathy. "Of course I'll be okay. You've been working your butt off lately. You need a break." He waved his hand toward the front door, shooing us away. "Off with you. I can hold the fort on my own. Relax and don't worry about a thing."

"There. That's settled." Ruby retrieved my handbag from underneath the counter and handed it to me. "Prepare to be healed!" She strode toward the door, holding my arm before I could object.

I gave a backward glance over my shoulder at Vernon, who smiled and gave me a thumbs-up.

"I didn't know anyone in town did crystal healing," I said as I slid into the passenger seat of Ruby's environmentally friendly Toyota Prius Hybrid.

"Oh, yes. I've known Pandora for years. She also does Reiki and Indian head massage too." She shifted the gearshift into drive and headed off down Craggy Hill toward town.

"Well, it's a great idea. Thank you for this." I'd had a couple of treatments when I was in India and thought the head massage was amazing. A spot of relaxation and rejuvenation was exactly what I needed.

"What are friends for?" She glanced over and gave me a coy look. "So, how are things going with Harvey? I saw him on the cliffs outside the tavern, excavating. How much has he managed to find so far?"

Although Harvey hadn't managed to find the remains of the *Ocean's Revenge* at sea yet, he had found the ship's bell. Together, we'd also found the entrance to some hidden caves used by the old smugglers, undiscovered since the ship sank in 1852. The caves ran underneath the cliffs outside the tavern and had preserved the gold, silver, and other smuggled items that were sought after at the time, like tea chests and alcohol, along with the skeletons of several of the smugglers who'd died the night the ship went down, trapped in a cavernous tomb with their booty. Harvey had been painstakingly recovering the loot, which was now safely ensconced at the University of Washington's Environment Studies Department in Seattle. Eventually, it would be part of a huge joint exhibition between Seattle and the Portsmouth Naval Museum, where Harvey worked. He was now bringing up the bones of the smugglers before he could turn his attention back to searching for the wreck.

"Things are going great with Harvey." I smiled as I thought about his vivid blue eyes that sparkled when he smiled, the cute British accent, those full lips—think Tom Hardy!—and his fun sense of humor and easy laugh. "Better than great, actually. He's been showing me some of the artifacts he's salvaged. It's amazing. Bob would've loved to see them." I sighed wistfully. Bob had always loved the history of Danger Cove, especially the smuggling angle that the town's roots were founded on.

Ruby patted my knee. "Bob would've loved Harvey, too, if he'd met him."

"Yes." I watched the town speed by out of the window and allowed myself a smile as I thought about my former friend. "He would."

"He's The One."

"The one, what?" I glanced back at her.

"The One! Harvey. He's your destiny."

I shook my head. "It's too early to tell that. We're just enjoying getting to know each other at the moment." Even though I didn't want to say it aloud in case I managed to mess things up, I'd been thinking the same thing a lot myself lately.

"Mark my words." She grinned, slowing down and parking on a quiet street in front of a gray-fronted, two-story house. There were large dormer windows on the second level and a porch contained by white railings that had faded in parts to the same color as the house.

We watched the front door of the house open, and Ruby let out a shocked, "Oh!" She stared, her jaw slack, at a guy exiting the front door wearing a well-cut charcoal suit and white shirt.

The man was definitely in a hurry, and he looked...well, either ill or in shock. His black hair was swept back, exposing a widow's peak at his forehead, and even from this angle I could see the sun reflecting a sheen of sweat on his pale skin. His eyes darted around wildly as he half ran, half stumbled down the path and onto the street. He didn't seem to notice us as he turned left and headed along the road that would take him back into town.

Now I was having second thoughts about the crystal healing session. Whatever Pandora had done to this guy didn't seem to have made him feel any better when he left.

"I don't believe it!" Ruby said, still staring in the direction the man had gone, even though he'd now disappeared.

"What?" I frowned.

"That was..." She trailed off, chewing on her lower lip.

"Who?"

"Tim."

I shrugged. His name wasn't familiar to me. I'd only been in town just over a year, and most of that time I'd been working, so I really only knew the regulars who came into the tavern. Plus, I was kind of a loner and enjoyed my own company. I'd had to be, all those years of being neglected growing up. Ruby and Vernon were my only close friends here, which suited me fine. I was happy with what I had. Ruby, on the other hand, seemed to know just about everyone in town.

"Tim who?"

"Tim Baxtor. He owns Baxtor's Pharmacy at the far end of Main Street. What was he doing here?" Ruby's gaze drifted to Pandora's front door, which Tim had left slightly ajar in his haste to get away.

I shifted in my seat and waved a hand in front of Ruby's glazed eyes. "What? What's going on?"

Ruby was silent for a while, lost in her own thoughts. "Tim Baxtor..." she started, then trailed off again.

I waited for her to carry on, but she didn't, so I turned to look at the house again, giving her a moment to collect herself.

Ruby finally sprang to attention, unbuckling her seat belt and almost springing out of the car like a caged cougar with the promise of freedom. "I've got to check on Pandora."

Confused, I followed her up the path. Judging by Ruby's expression, this Tim Baxtor person seemed like bad news.

Ruby knocked on the partially open door. "Hello? Pandora? Are you there?"

No reply.

Ruby pushed the door open further. It creaked ominously as it swung an arc, hitting the wall behind. "Pandora?" She stepped into a large hallway with a worn and slightly grubby oatmeal-colored carpet. "Pandora? Are you okay?"

We were still met with silence.

Ruby glanced at me. "Something's wrong."

"Do you think that guy has done something to Pandora?" I asked again.

She flapped a hand to silence me and rushed to the first door on the right, which was closed. She pushed it open so hard she almost fell flat on her face with the momentum. I glanced around. It was a living room with two old, faded floral sofas opposite each other. There were photos of a beautiful young blonde woman in frames on every available surface.

Ruby turned and bumped into me, then rushed to the room opposite, swinging the door open. "Pandora? Where are you?"

Before I had time to have a look over her shoulder, she was off again, heading toward an archway that led to the kitchen at the back of the house.

"Oh no!" Ruby's hands flew to her cheeks, and she stopped in her tracks by the fridge. "Pandora!"

I stepped through the archway and saw what she was looking at.

A very thin, petite woman was slumped over a teak dining table, bent over from the waist, her forehead resting on the table.

Ruby was frozen to the spot, so I ran toward Pandora. I'd learned first aid when I was volunteering at a Thai hospital after the horrific Tsunami in 2004, so I pressed my fingertips to her neck, feeling for a pulse. There wasn't one, but her skin was still warm. Gently, I lifted Pandora's torso so I could get a better look. Her eyes were wide open in a death stare. She wasn't breathing. There was a syringe with a small amount of liquid still inside stuck in the vein at her elbow. A glass vial was on the table, and under her chair was an empty plastic syringe wrapper.

"Call 9-1-1," I shouted, which seemed to spur Ruby into action.

She fumbled in her bag to pull out her cell phone, speaking into it in short, sharp bursts.

I maneuvered Pandora onto her back on the floor, kneeling next to her to perform CPR, the chair she'd been sitting on clattering down beside us. Placing one hand over the center of her chest and the other on top, I used my upper body weight to perform chest compressions. There were still no signs of life, so using a head tilt, I gently lifted her chin to open her airway. She wasn't breathing. I gave one mouth-to-mouth rescue breath, pinching her nostrils shut. Her chest didn't rise, so I gave another, then resumed chest compressions, arms aching, adrenaline coursing wildly through me, before going through another cycle of breathing.

When I saw two paramedics rush into the room, I finally sat back onto my heels and blew away a braid of hair that had become plastered to my forehead with sweat. I told them how we'd found her and what medical intervention I'd done, and they took over.

"Poor Pandora." Ruby shook her head while the paramedics worked on her.

I hugged Ruby toward me and watched until they stopped, knowing any further attempts to revive her were futile. Finally, they stood. One of them spoke into his radio while I wondered what had happened to Pandora. A drug overdose? Was she diabetic and miscalculated her insulin? No, that couldn't be right since the needle was in her vein. Whatever it was, I hoped it was quick and painless for her.

My gaze caught on the two tumbler glasses sitting on top of the table next to the glass vial. One was half full of clear liquid. Another, in front of where Pandora's head had been resting, was empty, but the remnants of the same liquid coated the glass. An almost empty bottle of white rum stood in the middle of the table.

"Police are on their way," one of the paramedics said to us as they packed away their equipment.

"Police." Ruby nodded vaguely, then sniffed. "It was Tim. I know it. Tim Baxtor killed her. He was just here."

"We don't know what's happened yet. You'll need to talk to the officers when they get here," the other one said. "I'm sorry for your loss."

I noticed the rear patio door that led to the garden was open. Suddenly wanting to gulp in some fresh air and get away from the sad sight of Pandora, I grabbed Ruby's hand, which was cold, and pulled her into the garden, being careful not to touch anything else. "Let's wait out here." I guided her into a gray mesh chair around a glass-topped table under an umbrella. "Why do you think it's this Tim person?" I asked Ruby. "Why would he want to hurt Pandora?"

"It's a long story." Ruby bit her lip.

I squeezed her hand.

"About twenty years ago, Pandora's daughter, Jenna, disappeared. I wasn't in town at the time. I was at a yoga retreat in Bali when it happened, and I didn't know Pandora at that time. It was years later when I met her, after she began doing her holistic treatments again, probably ten years ago or so."

I sat down next to Ruby.

"Anyway, Jenna was engaged to Tim Baxtor, but apparently she was having second thoughts about him and had decided to break it off. It was the night of the Danger Cove Fourth of July fair, so most of the people were on the other side of town in Main Street, where various stalls and attractions had been set up and fireworks were going off. Jenna told Pandora she was going to meet Tim and tell him it was over between them. Then she'd catch up with her back at the fair. But Jenna never returned. No one ever saw her again."

I gasped. And before Ruby could say anymore, my worst nightmare appeared.

CHAPTER TWO

Detective Lester Marshall. Great.

When I'd found Bob's body, Lester was convinced I'd murdered him to gain access to his fortune. Lester had done everything he could to try to pin it on me, and I'd nearly ended up singing the "Jailhouse Rock" in a hideous orange prison jumpsuit. Now here I was again, at the scene of another death. One that my fingerprints would now be all over.

Uh-oh!

"Well, well, well. Look what we have here." Lester headed toward me with his usual obnoxious swagger. If he were an animal, he'd be a gorilla—short, chunky, thick neck, macho. Maybe just a little less hairy though. "Another suspicious death, and you're in the thick of it again. You're like some kind of death magnet."

See, what did I tell you about the whole death-magnet thing?

He jabbed a stubby finger in my direction with a triumphant gleam in his eye. I could practically hear the cogs of his brain turning as he was working out how to pin this one on me, too, so he could notch up another arrest and get back to reading the paper and drinking coffee.

My stomach lurched up to my throat. "Yes, well, we can explain what we're doing here." I stood up, forcing myself to exude confidence.

He folded his arms in front of his chest, and I noticed a stain of what looked like black-currant jelly on the elbow of his shirt. A few crumbs adhered to his chin. "I can't wait to hear all about it." He raised mocking eyebrows at me.

"Oh, don't be so ridiculous, Detective." Ruby glared at him. "We both arrived and found Pandora like that."

"You don't say?" Lester tilted his head, giving us a *this should be good* expression.

"I *do* say, actually." Ruby's lifted her chin defiantly.

"Well, I'm all ears."

"Um...can I sit down again?" I nodded toward the chair. The adrenaline from trying to save Pandora had worn off, and I was trembling.

Lester pulled out a chair and sat down. He leaned back and resumed his arm-crossing position, giving me the beady eye. "Right. What's your story? How come you turned up at a second suspicious death in the space of two months?"

"We were due for a crystal healing appointment with Pandora at four," Ruby started. "As we pulled up outside, we saw Tim Baxtor leaving the house in a hurry. He looked...I don't know, a bit crazed."

"Crazed?" Lester looked pointedly at me, as if I knew all about being "crazed." "Right. Then what happened?"

"Well, I was in shock at seeing him there, and I was trying to get my head round it for a moment, so we sat in the car for a little while. Oh no!" She threw her head in her hands. "If only we'd gone in sooner, we might've been able to save her. It was my fault."

"It wasn't your fault," I said, rubbing Ruby's back. "You couldn't have known what was going on inside the house." I turned to Lester. "When we rushed inside, we found Pandora in the kitchen. She was slumped over the table, and I couldn't feel a pulse. I managed to get her on the floor and attempted CPR, but she was already dead."

"And you knew she was already dead, how? Did you kill her?"

"Of course not!"

"Weren't you listening?" Ruby dropped her hands to her lap. "Usually, when there's no pulse, it means someone is dead."

"We'll see about that. Are you both doctors?"

"Um...no." I clenched and unclenched my fists to try to stop them from shaking.

"Exactly." Lester placed his elbows on the table and leaned forward, keeping eye contact with me.

"It's not us you need to speak to," Ruby said. "It's Tim Baxtor. He was here just before we found her, and Pandora and Tim didn't get along."

Lester turned his attention to Ruby. "Really? And why is that?"

"It's a long story, and an old one."

Lester jerked his head in the direction of the house. "It looks like Pandora's not going anywhere at the moment, so I think we've got time for you to tell me."

Ruby narrowed her eyes at his insensitivity. "Twenty years ago Pandora's daughter, Jenna, disappeared."

"And why is that relevant?" Lester looked bored.

"If you'll let me *finish*, I'll tell you why."

Lester waved a hand for her to continue.

"Tim was engaged to Jenna, but she started having second thoughts about their relationship. She was going to break things off with him, but then she disappeared suddenly and was never heard from again. Detective Ohlsen investigated, and he couldn't find any evidence of foul play, but Pandora always believed Tim Baxtor had killed Jenna."

Lester whistled, looking intrigued. His eyes gleamed with excitement. Knowing him, he was probably thinking how he had a nice open-and-shut case he could tie up before the next round of donuts. "I never heard that story."

"You were probably in diapers when it happened," Ruby said. "Anyway, over the years, I think Bud kept an eye out in case there was ever any trace of Jenna, but nothing happened. She'd just vanished."

"How awful," I said.

"Consequently, Pandora hated Tim and publicly accused him in the past of murdering her daughter," Ruby carried on. "So there's absolutely no way he should have been here. *And* when we saw him practically running away, he looked highly suspicious. He must've somehow killed Pandora to shut her up once and for all."

At that moment the medical examiner, Catherine Cooper, came to the patio doors. She spotted Lester, and a flash of irritation crossed her face. Even she thought he was an ass. She took a breath of what looked like resignation and walked toward us. "Detective." She gave him a curt nod of acknowledgement, then looked between Ruby and me. "I understand one of you found the body and performed CPR?"

"Yes, that was me."

"Can you show me exactly what position she was in when you found her and what you did?"

"Of course." We all followed her into the kitchen, and I explained what we'd seen and what I'd done.

Catherine asked a few questions to clarify and then nodded before kneeling down to examine the body.

Ruby looked away from Pandora's lifeless body.

"What time did you arrive?" Lester asked us.

"Just before four," I said. "That's when our appointment was."

"And tell me again what that therapy thing was?"

"Crystal healing," Ruby said.

"Crystal what?" Lester frowned. "What the hell's that kind of freakery? What's wrong with going to a doctor or pharmacist when you're ill?"

Ruby sighed and looked as if she'd like to batter Lester with a very large, very heavy crystal. "Since Tim Baxtor is a pharmacist, probably a lot."

"So Pandora was a drug addict?" Lester eyed the needle in Pandora's vein.

"Stop jumping to conclusions again, Detective." Ruby sighed. "Pandora was into healthy, holistic treatments. I never knew her to take anything other than herbal remedies for things. She was most definitely not a drug addict."

Catherine sat back on her heels and glanced at the kitchen table. She picked up the empty tumbler with a gloved hand and stared into it with deep concentration before taking a sniff. She picked up the glass vial on the floor and read the label.

"I don't know why you're wasting time talking to us," Ruby said. "You need to get out there and find Tim Baxtor."

Her voice dragged my gaze back to Lester.

"This is my investigation," he said. "So we'll be doing things in my time."

God help us!

"Did Mr. Baxtor leave on foot or by vehicle?"

"On foot."

"And you say he looked agitated and suspicious?"

"Yes, very," Ruby replied.

The cogs in Lester's brain squeaked again for a moment before he said, "Okay, you can go. For now. Don't leave town. I'll need to speak to you again."

Oh, what joy. I can't wait.

Just as Ruby and I walked down the hallway, I heard Catherine's voice, loud and clear, saying, "I won't know the cause of death for certain until I do the postmortem and toxicology, but this stuff is lethal."

CHAPTER THREE

———

By the time Ruby and I got back to Smugglers' Tavern, the dinner crowd was in full swing, and we only had time to have a quick chat with Vernon and let him know what had happened, before we were rushed off our feet. At 9:30 p.m. the crowd was filtering away, and I sat down on a stool behind the bar, giving my feet a much-needed rest while I waited for Ruby and Vernon to join me. The front door opened, and I glanced in that direction, my breath catching in my throat.

Harvey.

He gave me a cheeky, lopsided grin that made my heart beat a little faster, and for a second, he made me forget about the horrors of the day. He rounded the bar and pulled me in toward him. I melted into his firm chest. As always, he smelled of the sea and outdoors—earthy and briny, mixed with his unique Harvey scent.

"I missed you." He kissed me on the lips.

"Missed you too." I held on tight, closing my eyes and savoring the tingling that erupted inside.

"How was your day?"

"Pretty awful, actually. Ruby and I discovered one of her friends who'd died. It's likely she was murdered." I explained what had happened as Harvey's eyes widened.

"Blimey! That's terrible. Ruby must be gutted." In Harvey's Brit lingo, that meant devastated. He squeezed me tighter. "Are you okay? Must've been a big shock for you both."

"I will be. I didn't know Pandora, but I like to believe she's gone to a much happier place now. How was your day?"

"Busy again, as usual. There's still so much to recover from the caves, and I can't wait to get back out in the ocean and search for the ship. I spoke to Steve, my boss at Portsmouth Naval Museum, and he thinks he can spare another member of our department to come over and help. They should be here in the next few days, which is wicked news."

"Oh, that's great!" I said.

Ruby joined us behind the bar, and Vernon, whose shift was now over, sat on the opposite side. Ruby had a faraway look in her eye.

"Earth to Ruby." Vernon waved a hand in front of her face.

She twisted in her seat to face us. "Sorry, I was just thinking about Pandora and Jenna. I can't imagine how terrible it would be not knowing what happened to your daughter all these years. I mean, even if Tim did kill Jenna, wouldn't it be better to actually know that, rather than wondering and hoping that one day she could walk through the door?"

"It would eat you up inside," I said. "At least if you knew for certain, you could go through the grieving process."

"So do you really think Tim Baxtor killed Pandora?" Harvey asked.

I shrugged. "We don't know. She'd been pumped full of some kind of drug. The syringe was still in her arm. We saw Tim leave the house just before we found her, and he's a pharmacist with access to all sorts of stuff. And obviously they had some unpleasant history between them. The ME said what she found was lethal. It sounds like she might've been poisoned."

"Exactly," Ruby said. "He must've done it. Otherwise, why would he have been there? Pandora would never have let him in the house."

"Catherine Cooper will probably finish the postmortem by tomorrow morning," Vernon said. "I'll get in touch with my contact at Seattle PD and find out the results. But it does seem highly suspicious, going by what you've told us." From Vernon's FBI days, he had contacts in law enforcement agencies all over the place.

Harvey's brow knitted at Vernon. He wasn't aware of Vernon's past, and it wasn't my secret to tell. "What kind of contact?"

"One of the parents of the kids I used to teach works there," Vernon said without missing a beat.

"Oh, right." Harvey pursed his sexy lips with a thoughtful expression. "Well, I don't know about you, but I think I need a drink after hearing all this terrible news." He drummed his fingers lightly on the bar.

I grabbed a bottle of cider from the fridge and filled a glass with ice, placing it in front of him.

"Couldn't agree with you more," Vernon said. "I'll try one of those Smugglers' coladas, please."

"I thought you stopped drinking!" Ruby said.

It was no secret Vernon liked a drink. Before he began helping me out in the tavern, he was usually propped up on the other side of the bar every night. He was a happy, fun drunk, though, and after hearing some of the things he'd been through in his time at the FBI, I couldn't really blame him. He'd been shot in the knee in the line of duty and in considerable pain for a long time. When the painkillers didn't work anymore, he'd turned to booze. The only thing that had stopped him drinking was when we'd been investigating Bob's murder and he needed to have a clear head. But in the last few weeks, he'd slipped back into his old habits.

Vernon shrugged. "And now I started again."

Ruby shot him a worried look. She opened her mouth to say something, but Vernon cut her off.

"You're not my mother, so don't look at me like that."

"No, but I am a friend, and I worry about you." She rested a manicured hand on his arm and gave a gentle squeeze.

Vernon glanced down at her hand for a moment, a wistful look on his face. He placed his over hers and patted gently. "I know what I'm doing."

"You need a distraction again to stop you drinking," Ruby said decisively.

"No, I need a Smugglers' colada." Vernon looked up at me expectantly.

I sighed. I worried about his drinking too. With alcoholic parents, it stayed on my mind a lot. And it was ironic that I'd ended up owning a bar. But Vernon was a big boy, and I was a bartender. As much as you like to help your friends, you can't live your life for them.

The door opened, and Duncan Pickles, hack reporter extraordinaire, walked in wearing a rumpled suit. I recognized him from his byline photo in the *Cove Chronicles*. He zeroed in on Ruby and me behind the bar and waltzed over.

"Hi, Duncan Pickles from the local paper. I heard you two found Pandora Williams today." Holding his hand out to me, his eyes gleamed with the sniff of a good story.

I ignored his hand, so he swung it in Ruby's direction. There was no way I was talking to a reporter about what I'd seen, especially one as unscrupulous as him.

"I've got nothing to say to you." Ruby glared at his hand like it was poisonous. "Knowing you, you'll put some kind of nasty slant on things. Pandora should be able to rest in peace." She pointed toward the door, her silver mandala bracelet jangling. "You know the way out."

Duncan shrugged casually. "You know I'm going to report it anyway, so you might as well tell me what happened." He swung back to me again. "So?"

"So, what?"

"How did you find her? What position was the body in? How did Tim Baxtor look when he was running away from the scene?"

I held a hand up to silence him. "You won't get anything out of me. I've got no comment."

"But you think he's guilty, right? I mean, no one else could've got into that house and killed her, could they? It's pretty impossible. So, I heard some kind of drug was used to bump her off. What do you think it was?"

"Right, that's it." Vernon grabbed hold of the collar on Duncan's jacket and steered him toward the door.

"Hey! That's assault, that is! I'm only doing my job."

"Well, go and do it somewhere else. You heard the ladies. They're not talking to you." Vernon opened the door and calmly ejected Duncan. Then wiped his hands down his trousers, as if Duncan had contaminated him with scum, before heading back toward us.

Two hours later, I closed up the tavern and flicked off the lights. Harvey followed me down the private corridor behind the bar and along the internal entrance to the apartment above. I unlocked the door and found Zen, my black tomcat, sitting behind the door, waiting for me with a look on his face as if to say *where've you been, human? I'm starving!*

I scooped him up in my arms and kissed his head.

"Where's Karma?" Harvey asked, closing the door behind me as we walked up the stairs that led into an open plan lounge/kitchen. There were windows along the length of the front wall facing the ocean. Sometimes I'd sit here and just stare at the waves, trying to empty my mind of thoughts and just meditate on the ever-changing scenery. It was amazing how the sea never stayed the same color. It seemed to have moods, just like humans. Some days it was fiery and argumentative, some days tranquil and easygoing.

Hearing his name, Karma's head popped up from behind the tiny sofa that I'd brought with me from the cottage. It looked ridiculously small in the large room, but Elise and Carter had sneaked in one night and removed all of Bob's furniture to sell, and even though they didn't have the right to do that since he'd left his estate to me, I didn't want to rock the boat by challenging them over it. With what Bob had left me, I could buy a million sofas and still have change. When the estate was all finally settled, I was going to be a rich woman. I still couldn't get my head around that. I needed to do some serious thinking about what to do with all that money. I knew I was going to donate some to the Second Chance Animal Rescue center, but apart from that, I didn't have a clue yet.

Harvey slumped on the sofa and moved Karma onto his lap. Karma rolled onto his back, offering Harvey his soft belly, and meowed until Harvey gave the obligatory stroke. Even though he only had three legs—Karma, not Harvey—it didn't seem to deter him from being a normal, agile cat. After he'd found his way into my life, I'd taken him to the vet for a checkup and to start his inoculations, and the vet said he was perfectly healthy. I curled up next to Harvey, resting my head on his shoulder, savoring the moment alone. With both our work schedules lately, it had been hard to get any private time together. Zen, determined not to be left out, sat in between us, nudging me with his head.

Harvey laughed, exposing that sexy dimple on his right cheek. You could tell a lot about a man by how he treated animals, and I felt a warm rush of contentment as I watched him talking to Karma as he rubbed the cat's belly gently. I was pretty sure I was falling in love.

CHAPTER FOUR

———

"Pandora was killed with pentobarbital," Vernon said as soon as he walked through the door of the tavern. It was just after 9:00 a.m., and I was retrieving cutlery from the dishwasher and winding napkins around it. "I just got off the phone with my contact."

Ruby stopped wiping down the tables and gasped. "So it's true. Tim killed Pandora?" She walked toward us, hand on hip, an angry red flush creeping up her neck. "That poor woman. After all she went through with Jenna."

"What's pentobarbital?" I asked, mouth agape.

"It's a barbiturate," Vernon said. "It's used for several things, like treating seizures, but most importantly, it's used in the euthanasia of humans and animals. It's been used a lot as a lethal injection for death penalty cases. Administered intravenously, death is pretty much instantaneous."

"How awful." Ruby slumped onto a barstool. "I just hope it was painless and she didn't suffer."

"Lester Marshall has arrested Tim Baxtor," Vernon said.

"But if Tim had administered the drug intravenously, how did he get Pandora to sit still long enough to stick a needle in her?" I said. "Surely she would've put up a fight."

"There were no defense wounds mentioned in the autopsy report," Vernon said. "And no traces of any other drugs in her system, like a sedative. There were also no other injuries that might've rendered her unconscious first."

"So how did he manage it, then?" My forehead crinkled. "Surely she would've been struggling."

"Unless she was asleep," Ruby said.

"At the kitchen table?" I asked.

Vernon shrugged. "I've been known to nod off on the odd occasion there."

"Yes, that's because you were drunk, most probably." Ruby quirked an eyebrow.

I remembered the bottle of rum on the table. "How much alcohol did they find in her system?" I asked.

"She was way over the legal driving limit, so that might explain it," Vernon said.

"Maybe she'd been drinking the rum all afternoon. The bottle was almost empty," I said.

"But we don't know when she bought it," Vernon said.

"True, but she'd obviously been drinking a hefty dose of something alcoholic." I put the cutlery on a tray underneath the bar.

"I think Tim must've got inside Pandora's house, found her passed out, and stuck the drug in her vein." Ruby's eyes flashed with sadness. "And obviously the police must think the same if Tim's been arrested."

"That doesn't make sense," Vernon scoffed. "What? You think Tim just happened to walk around all the time with a vial of pentobarbital and a syringe in his pocket, hoping for the off-chance to whack someone? How did he get inside the house in the first place if, like you say, Pandora wouldn't have let him in?"

"The back door was open. He could've got in that way," I said.

"Then kill Pandora and walk out the front door in broad daylight?" Vernon shook his head.

"Why not?" Ruby asked. "Criminals do some dumb things sometimes."

Vernon rubbed his chin between his thumb and forefinger, deep in thought. I noticed the same spark of intrigue and excitement in his eyes I'd seen when we were investigating Bob's death. I guessed it must be hard to be a special agent all your working life, then give it up and do nothing. Vernon seemed to come alive again at the hint of a challenge, especially one that involved investigating a murder.

"Did Pandora have any other family?" I asked.

"Yes." Ruby nodded. "She had a son, Ian, although they've been estranged for years. Not surprisingly, when Jenna went missing, Pandora sank into a depression. She was obsessed with finding out what happened to her daughter and couldn't think of anything else. I guess Ian felt neglected, and they drifted apart. I didn't know Pandora well at the time, so I've never met him. Ian left town a few years after Jenna disappeared, and I don't think he's been back since." Ruby poured herself a bottle of water, added a slice of lemon, and took a sip. "Pandora had such tragedy in her life. First, she lost her husband to an aneurysm ten years before Jenna disappeared, then she lost her daughter, and eventually her relationship with Ian broke down. After Jenna, Pandora became kind of a recluse, spending most of her time in the house. She didn't really get involved with other people, apart from the healing treatments. She seemed to be able to help other people but was totally unable to help herself.

"She trained to be a nurse at first before taking up holistic therapy, but she was far too down after Jenna to carry on working for a long time. From what she told me, she could hardly get up in the mornings for years. Her husband was very wealthy, so at least she'd had the family money to fall back on."

I pictured Pandora's modest three-bedroom home with the outdated and worn furniture and lack of new technology or equipment. It didn't look as if she'd modernized it in years, so I wondered briefly what she'd done with her money.

"So if Tim did kill Jenna, not only did he ruin one life, he ruined three," I said. "Ian must've been just as devastated as Pandora when Jenna went missing."

"I wonder how Ian's taking things now," Ruby said. "Even though he and Pandora didn't have a good relationship any longer, she was still his mom. Maybe I should get hold of his number and phone him. Make sure he's okay. Give him my condolences at least. I could help him arrange the funeral. I feel like I should be doing something useful."

I smiled at my friend who had a heart of gold. She was fiercely loyal. "That's a nice idea. Ian's welcome to have the wake here, if he likes. I doubt very much he'd want to hold it at Pandora's house, after she died there. Tara and Clara can easily handle the catering."

"Good idea. I'll phone Lester and get hold of Ian's number."

"Hmmm, rather you than me." I'd rather have my appendix taken out than talk to Lester. "Do you really think Tim did it? Jenna, I mean?"

"I guess we'll never know for certain, but it is very suspicious that Jenna was never heard from again," Vernon said.

"Exactly," Ruby agreed.

"It would be easy to get rid of a body here." Vernon glanced through the window toward the ocean. "We're surrounded by water. You could just take a boat out, weigh the body down, and throw it overboard. It would be fish food in no time, and the skeleton would be scattered everywhere with these tides. Just look at the trouble Harvey's having locating the rest of the *Ocean's Revenge*."

I shuddered, a sudden image of Jenna being picked apart by sharks and fishes popping into my head. I blinked it away. What a sad story.

The front door opened, and Tara, the recently promoted chef, walked in, laden with some bags of produce and closely followed by Clara. Luckily, they weren't identical twins, so I could easily tell them apart. Tara was tall and slim, with a shock of red curls. Clara was the opposite. Short and slightly overweight with fine, lank, black short hair.

"Morning all!" They both said together. They did have a tendency to say the same things at the same times and finish off each other's sentences.

Vernon slid off the stool and limped toward them, taking the bags. "Let me give you a hand."

"Thanks." Tara gave us a huge smile. "Okay, so today I'm doing grilled miso salmon with rice noodles, and honey and orange sea bass with Le Puy lentils, as the specials," she said to me. "What do you think?"

The specialty of the tavern was its fresh, locally sourced seafood. "Sounds yum." I licked my lips. "I'll write it on the board out front."

Tara looked at us expectantly. "Anyone want a—"

"BLT before we start?" Clara finished off for her.

Tara carried on as if nothing had happened. I guess she was used to it, but it could be a bit disconcerting sometimes. "I can rustle up some breakfast for you before we start our—"

"Prep work," Clara finished. "Sounds like you've had a busy—"

"Time of it," Tara butted in. "What with finding poor Pandora and all."

Ruby gave them both a look of horror. "I'm vegan."

Tara waved a hand through the air. "Oh. Yeah, sorry. I forgot. You want an LT sandwich instead?"

"No, I'll pass, thanks," Ruby said.

"Anyone else up for a sandwich, then?" Clara and Tara said at the same time.

"Not for me, thanks," I said. "I've eaten." I'd already been up for ages, doing an hour's yoga and meditation before polishing off some organic muesli and almond milk.

"Not that rabbit food healthy stuff again." Tara chuckled at me.

"I'll have one. No, make that two." Vernon disappeared into the kitchen with the bags. "Heavy on the bacon, mayonnaise, and ketchup," he shouted.

"You're going to die of a heart attack one day!" Ruby called after him.

"What about Harvey?" Tara jerked her thumb in the direction of outside. "Shall I make him one too? He looks like—"

"He could do with something to warm him up," Clara finished. "That wind's—"

"Freezing today," Tara added.

"I'm sure he'd love that," I said, not quite knowing which one to answer.

We busied ourselves for opening, until the food was ready, and Tara plonked two plates of sandwiches onto the bar.

Vernon sat down and picked up a slice of bread, seeing how much mayonnaise and ketchup were underneath. It was obviously lacking the Vernon taste test as he grabbed a bottle of mayo and squeezed a heavy dollop on both his sandwiches. Satisfied they were drowned in gloop, he studied the mammoth item, looking for the best angle to stuff it in without it falling apart. Ruby shook her head at him as he tucked in.

I wandered outside to find Harvey, making my way through the tavern's garden and over to a privacy tent that had been erected over the excavated entrance to the caves. I poked my head inside but couldn't see him. On the ground inside the entrance was a large plastic sheet weighted down at each corner with large rocks. Several human bones with a light layer of earth had been placed in a large plastic box. I stared at the bones, a chill running through me as I wondered again what had really happened to Jenna.

"Oh, hi!" Harvey poked his head out of the entrance to the cave and climbed up a ladder he'd placed there. His hands were gloved, and he was holding a mesh basket filled with what looked like finger bones.

"Hey." I grinned. When Harvey was around, I couldn't help grinning. "There's a BLT with your name on it inside."

"Great. I'm dying for some grub. All this sea air makes you hungry."

"How are you getting on?" My gaze strayed to the bones again.

"Slowly. I'm finding more and more down here every day as I excavate through the collapsed cave." He removed his gloves and put them inside a hold-all bag, then fell into step beside me as we walked inside. I filled him in on Pandora being killed by pentobarbital and Tim being arrested.

"Wow. I'm getting a bit worried about this town. It's like being on a set of *Midsummer Murders*. I'm starting to realize why it's called Danger Cove. Do you think I'm safe here?" He shot me a coy look.

"Not from me." I giggled with a sly grin.

"I've got a mini crisis!" Tara popped her head out of the kitchen, a dusting of flour covering her hair. She slapped a palm to her head. "I can't believe I've run out of miso paste. Can someone pop out and get me some?"

"Sure," I said, retrieving my bag from under the bar. "Be back soon." I hopped onto my bicycle that was stashed behind the tavern and rode down Craggy Hill into town. I was just passing Cinnamon Sugar Bakery when I saw Detective Bud

Ohlsen coming out, laden with a bag of goodies, his salt-and-pepper hair shining in the sunlight. I wondered how many donuts were in there for Lester.

The few times I'd met Bud, he'd always struck me as methodical and competent, preferring to take his time with cases, examining all the evidence and not jumping to conclusions, unlike Lester.

I skidded to a stop next to his car. I hadn't been able to get Jenna's disappearance out of my mind, and if anyone had a guess as to what had really happened to her, it would be Bud, who'd worked the case.

I was just about to approach him when a tall, big-boned woman rushed up to him on the street with a Labrador on a leash. She was in her midforties, not overweight but very thickset, with thick glasses, her long brown hair mussed up in matted tangles, wearing lime-green sweatpants and a glaringly bright-red T-shirt, as if she'd thrown the mismatched clothes on in a hurry.

"Detective Ohlsen!" she cried out.

He stopped. Turned to face her.

"Tim's just called my cell and said he'd been arrested!" Her cheeks were pink, nostrils flared. "I was just out taking the dog for a walk, so I'm on my way as fast as I can. He said he needs a lawyer! What's going on? This is outrageous."

Bud steered the woman away from the entrance to the bakery and into a doorway of a closed shop, talking so quietly I couldn't hear anything else. I watched her body language, the arms flailing around, her eyes shining, her lips firing words at him. After a few minutes, she took a deep breath, then left him there and dashed up the street, dog in tow, heading in the direction of the police station. Bud stood watching her for a moment before approaching his car.

"Hi, Detective," I said.

"Hope." He nodded a greeting at me. "It sounds like you had a traumatic day yesterday."

"Yes. I've had better ones. I heard you arrested Tim Baxtor. Has he confessed yet?"

Bud scrunched up his mouth. "No. He says he's innocent."

"Was that his wife?" I asked.

"Yes, Donna Baxtor."

"So, do you think he's innocent?"

"It's not my case. Lester's dealing with it, so I haven't interviewed him. I wouldn't like to speculate at this stage."

"But you did investigate Jenna's disappearance, didn't you? What do you think really happened to her?"

Bud inhaled a deep breath and rocked back on his heels, glancing up at the sky, in deep thought for a moment before looking back at me. "It's still an open case, so I can't say too much. We searched everywhere we could think of in the area, and there was no trace of her." He stared at something over my shoulder with a pained and defeated expression. "It's one of those cases that haunt you, you know. I wanted to find an answer for Pandora. Give her some kind of closure. But that's not always possible. It wrecked her life. Wrecked her son's, Ian's life, too, really. The family was never the same again, not surprisingly."

"But it sounded as if Pandora thought Tim killed Jenna and got away with it. Why would he kill Pandora too?"

"We're still trying to ascertain what's happened." Bud scratched his head. "Poor woman. She had such a tragic life. It was like her family was cursed. Years ago, Pandora told anyone who would listen how it was Tim that killed Jenna. She went to the papers and camped outside Tim's parents' house with placards calling him a murderer. She had a daily vigil outside his pharmacy, telling anyone going in how Tim had gotten away with murder. She was consumed with it all. It took over her life. The problem was, since we couldn't find any evidence of any wrongdoing by Tim, it was Pandora that we had to keep arresting for disturbing the peace." He sighed. "It was a sorry state of affairs. Tim wanted charges filed against her, but no one had the heart to do it. Tim eventually got a restraining order against her, and she wasn't allowed to go anywhere near him or his business. He threatened to sue her for slander too."

"What happened then?"

"She stopped the protests. She just seemed to give up. She stopped her holistic practice for a long time and became kind of a recluse. We never had any more trouble from her demonstrations after that."

I mulled that over for a moment. If that was all over years ago, what kind of motive would Tim have for killing her now? Unless... "Do you think Pandora found out something about Jenna? Something that proved Tim really did kill her?"

He hesitated. "I can't really say. But if she did, she didn't come to me with it. Tim was a pharmacist. He had easy access to the drugs that were found in Pandora's system, and he was seen leaving the house shortly after her death. On the surface it seems cut and dried."

I let his words sink in, thinking. It was almost *too* cut and dried. And judging from Bud's expression, he was thinking the same. There were plenty of ways to kill someone. Why make it so obviously point back to you? Why go to Pandora's house to kill her in the middle of the day when there could be witnesses around? Why not sneak in there under cover of night and make it look like a burglary gone wrong? And why use a drug that Tim could so easily get hold of? Then again, maybe Tim Baxtor was an idiot. Although if he'd killed once and got away with it, I very much doubted it.

CHAPTER FIVE

———

The tavern was busy all afternoon, but Pandora's death and Jenna's disappearance weren't far from my mind. Since meeting Harvey, his passion for history and the study of people had rubbed off on me. It was now too late for Pandora to discover the truth about Jenna, or maybe she already had and she'd confronted Tim about some evidence she'd found, and that's why she'd been murdered. I couldn't help thinking that solving Jenna's decades-old disappearance would solve Pandora's death too, and I wanted to find out more about what had happened all those years ago. I didn't think it was likely Bud Ohlsen would give any more away if it was still technically an open case. And I'd rather be trapped in a room with a million mosquitoes than speak to Lester again. Who knew what he'd do if he found out I was poking around in his investigation.

I tried googling information, but since Jenna went missing in 1995 and the internet didn't really kick off until around 1999, all I found was a small follow-up piece from 2005 on the ten-year anniversary of her disappearance, saying there were no new leads.

Next stop, a trip to the Danger Cove Library to check out the archived news reports.

I asked the helpful library assistant, Amy Spannagel, if she could show me where the old newspapers were stored.

"Are you looking for something in particular?" Amy pushed her glasses up her nose with her fingertip.

"Yes, some news reports from July 4, 1995, onwards."

"They're all stored on microfiche. We wouldn't have enough space to house all the papers here, and we haven't got round to digitizing the old records yet. But I know exactly where those films will be. Follow me." She led me through the main library area to a small room at the end, pausing to shush a couple of teenagers who were sitting at a table, poring over a book and giggling.

Several desks had computer stations set up. There were two screens at one end set up for the microfiches.

"Okay." She headed toward a huge filing cabinet, quickly scanning the labels at the front, which were split into five-year periods. She pulled open the draw for 1990–1995 and handed me a few big boxes of films. "Do you know how to use the machine?"

"No."

"It's easy." She sat down, slid a film in, and the newspaper text appeared on screen. "Just turn this dial to move forward or back." She stood up. "If you have any problems, feel free to come and ask me."

"Great, thanks." I sat in the seat she'd vacated and flicked through the films, which had been labeled with the dates in the top right-hand corner in permanent marker.

Inserting the first one, I flicked through to July 5, 1995, the day after Jenna had disappeared.

Local Woman Missing

Danger Cove local Jenna Williams, aged 23, has been reported as missing following the annual Fourth of July celebrations last night. Police officers were alerted to her disappearance by her mother, Pandora Williams, who said Jenna had been enjoying the firework display on Main Street before she left to meet with her boyfriend, Tim Baxtor, at the Danger Cove Lighthouse.

Tim Baxtor, also a resident of Danger Cove, informed Pandora Williams when Jenna didn't arrive as planned at the meeting spot, and despite the two searching the town, no trace of Jenna was found.

An official missing person's report has now been filed, and police are looking for Jenna. If you have any information regarding Jenna Williams, please contact Detective Bud Ohlsen of the Danger Cove Police Department.

I flicked through to the next report, dated July 6.

Community Joins the Search for Missing Woman

Local volunteers from the Danger Cove community rallied with the police to search for missing woman Jenna Williams, but no trace of her has been found. Jenna's mother, Pandora Williams, spoke to us from her home late last night. Williams said, "The police think it's possible that Jenna ran away, but she would never do that without telling me. Something has happened to her. She told me she was meeting up with her boyfriend, Tim Baxtor, to end their three-year relationship, but Tim claims she never showed up. She didn't take anything with her that night, no clothes or driver's license or anything. Her bedroom is just as she left it." In an emotional plea, Williams said, "If anyone has any information about Jenna's whereabouts, please, please contact the police. I want her to come home safe and well."

When questioned by reporters, Tim Baxtor said he had "no idea" Jenna was intending to break up with him. "We were engaged and very happy," Baxtor said. "We were meeting at the lighthouse to get away from the crowds that night and have a romantic evening at the bluff, looking at the stars and planning our future. At first, when she didn't arrive, I wasn't too worried. Jenna was always late. But after I waited an hour, I knew something was wrong and immediately went back to Main Street, thinking Jenna had lost track of time and was still enjoying the celebrations. Pandora and I went searching for Jenna, but it wasn't until the early hours of the next morning when she didn't arrive back home that I really began to get worried. If anyone knows where she is or what's happened to her, please let us know."

I scrolled forward and found another report dated July 9.

Tim Baxtor Questioned in Connection with Missing Woman

Local pharmacist Tim Baxtor has been brought in for questioning following the disappearance of Jenna Williams. Jenna's mother, Pandora Williams, claims Jenna had been about to end her relationship when she went missing. Williams said, "Tim was becoming jealous and controlling, and Jenna wanted out. He didn't want her to take her dream job as a designer at a prestigious Seattle firm and leave town. Jenna went to meet Tim to break off their engagement, but she never turned up. I know something bad has happened to her. We were very close, and she'd never leave without saying good-bye."

And another report on July 10.

Tim Baxtor's Parents' House Searched for Signs of Jenna Williams

Police were searching the home of Tim Baxtor's parents yesterday for any sign of his missing fiancée, Jenna Williams. Baxtor lives with his parents, Colleen and Dave, who are currently holidaying in Antigua and are not available for comment. Detective Bud Ohlsen was not prepared to release any statement but said that "Tim Baxtor is helping us with our inquiries. We're searching a number of locations in town to see if we can find Jenna. I'm still hoping we'll find her alive and well. And if anyone has any knowledge of her disappearance, or has seen her, please contact me."
When questioned at his parents' house, Tim Baxtor said, "I haven't done anything wrong. I loved Jenna and would never hurt her. The police are just doing a thorough job in leaving no stone unturned. If you're reading this, Jenna, please get in touch. We all love and miss you."

The reports carried on over the coming weeks and months, rehashing what was already known, which was very little. No witnesses came forward reporting they'd seen Jenna. And no evidence had ever been found relating to her disappearance or finding her body. The next time Jenna's name cropped up was in relation to Pandora's protests outside Tim Baxtor's pharmacy, which began six months later. There was a photo of Pandora standing outside the building with a placard held high above her head, the words *Baxtor Killed My Daughter!* on it.

Pandora Williams Arrested During Protest

Pandora Williams, mother of missing Danger Cove woman, Jenna, has been arrested following a number of protests outside Tim Baxtor's pharmacy. There has been no sign of Jenna since she disappeared on the night of July 4, and Pandora believes Jenna's fiancé, Baxtor, is responsible for her death. Pandora claims that "Tim killed my daughter! He murdered her and got rid of her body so we'd never find her. I want the world to know what he's done! It's not fair that he's allowed to live his life when Jenna can't. I just want him to tell me what he's done with her. I need answers!" Pandora was led away by Detective Bud Ohlsen.

Tim Baxtor commented, "I'm innocent. I had nothing to do with Jenna's disappearance. I miss her as much as everyone and wish she'd return. I understand Pandora's grief, but I was cleared of any involvement, and I just want to pick up the pieces and get on with my life and business."

There were more protests by Pandora and more arrests over the following months, but Pandora was never charged with anything. The final report I found mentioned Tim Baxtor having had enough and threatening to sue Pandora for slander and libel if she carried on harassing him. His threats appeared to have the desired effect, and the protests stopped. That was probably when Pandora turned her anger inward and sank into a deep depression, neglecting Ian in the process.

* * *

Vernon's phone rang out a loud rock beat as I locked up the tavern at closing time. I was bushed, and a steaming hot bath with some lavender essential oil was calling my name. Harvey was in Seattle, having taken his latest finds there to catalogue and store at the university's research department, and he wouldn't be back until late. It was just me and the kitties tonight.

Ruby kissed me on both cheeks and said she was leaving, but Vernon held up a hand to stop her as he listened intently to whoever was talking on the other end of his phone.

Vernon hung up and turned to face us. "Well, that was interesting. According to my source in Seattle, Tim Baxtor has told Lester Marshall that he was set up. He said Pandora called him about midday out of the blue and asked him to come round at 3:30 p.m. that day. He hadn't heard from her for years and was reluctant to go there at first, but she said she had evidence about what had really happened to Jenna. So he said against his better judgment he went because he wanted to finally clear his name once and for all. When he got there, she let him in, and they sat in the kitchen. Apparently she was already pretty drunk, and she poured them both a glass of rum. He said he didn't touch his, but she was necking it back like it was tap water. Then instead of telling him she'd found out something, she got really angry, demanding that he tell her where Jenna's body was so she could finally say a proper good-bye."

"So he killed her to shut her up?" Ruby muttered.

Vernon shrugged. "He says not. He told Lester that Pandora wouldn't listen to him when he tried to explain he had nothing to do with Jenna's disappearance, so he walked out. He said she was very much alive when he left."

"Except we saw him leave, and when we got inside, she was dead," Ruby said.

"It was only a few minutes before we found her," I said. "Five at the most."

"I think he's lying," Ruby said.

There *were* two glasses of rum on the kitchen table—I thought back to the dreadful scene in the kitchen—along with the glass vial of what must've contained the pentobarbital.

"The toxicology report did say she had a lot of alcohol in her system, so she would've been impaired," Vernon said. "Tim could've overpowered her, grabbed her arm, and intravenously injected her full of the drug. If she was drunk, it would've been easy. He must've been wearing gloves, because the only prints found on the syringe, the plastic wrapper, and the vial were Pandora's, who probably tried to grab them off him when he was trying to kill her. And they didn't find any of his prints inside the house."

"Did they check the phone records to see if she had called Tim like he claimed?" I asked Vernon.

"Yeah, there's no such call listed at that time from Pandora's landline, and as far as they know, she didn't have a cell. But..." He held up a finger for emphasis. "There was a two-minute call made to Tim's cell from an unregistered pay-as-you-go phone at the time he stated."

I let that sink in. Something didn't seem right to me. "But it all sounds too neat, doesn't it?" I chewed on my lip.

"But who else would've killed her?" Ruby asked. "Who else had a motive or opportunity?"

"I agree with Hope. Something's not quite adding up." Vernon paced up and down. "If you're going to kill someone, then you want to make sure it doesn't point back to you. The use of pentobarbital and the fact Tim was in that house in broad daylight seems too obvious to me."

"That's exactly what I thought," I said. "Can't they find out exactly where the call was made from?"

"There's only one cell tower in Danger Cove. The only thing they can be sure of is that the call to Tim was made from this town," Vernon said.

"But no one else could've slipped inside the kitchen and done it," Ruby said. "We saw Tim leaving in a big hurry, and five minutes later, we found her body."

"Unless someone else got in through the back door?" Vernon suggested. "You know the layout of her house. Could anyone gain access through the rear? Could they get in and out unnoticed?"

Ruby tapped her fingernails on the bar, thinking. "The rear patio door that led into the kitchen was open. And her garden backs onto a secluded wooded area. I guess someone else could've climbed the five-foot fence, then came in and out before we got inside, but that's highly unlikely."

"What about the son? Ian?" Vernon asked. "By all accounts, Pandora had money from her husband's business. Who stood to inherit from her?"

"As far as I know, the only surviving relative is Ian. I phoned him earlier," Ruby said. "He seemed genuinely shocked about what had happened. He lives in Seattle but said he was driving down early tomorrow morning to make the funeral arrangements. He said he'd speak to you about arranging the wake here," she said to me.

"Seattle's not that far," Vernon said. "He could've easily got down here and back to bump her off. What does he do for a living?"

"Um...he's a doctor," Ruby said. "A cardiologist who works at a private practice."

"A doctor? That means he could've got hold of the pentobarbital too," I said. I'd been convinced that Pandora's death was linked somehow to Jenna's, but maybe not. Maybe it was just about greed, and Ian wanted some of Pandora's money.

"Perhaps Tim's telling the truth, then," Vernon said. "Perhaps he really was set up."

CHAPTER SIX

———

I was awakened early by a banging on my door. The apartment had two entrances, one internal door with access from the tavern, and one that led directly out to the side of the building. This is where the noise was coming from. I dislodged Zen from his usual lounging position around the top of my head, and he gave me an indignant huff. I was hoping it was Harvey. I'd been having a very nice dream where Harvey and I had been traveling on the *Ocean's Revenge*, when it had sunk just off a deserted island in the middle of the Caribbean. Karma and Zen were with us too, and we all managed to make it to the golden shores, sheltering under the lush mango trees and banana plants as we worked together to build a house while the cats caught us fish for dinner, heading out to sea with their snorkels and masks on, which was a bit weird. At night we made love under the moonlit sky, stars so abundant it seemed as if they were falling into the sea on the horizon.

Unfortunately, it wasn't Harvey at the door. It was Lester Marshall. Bummer.

"Oh, hi." I leaned on the doorframe, wiping my eyes.

"I need to ask you some more questions."

"Right." I stepped back. "You'd better come in."

He followed me up the stairs into the lounge and glanced around disapprovingly. At one time he'd been involved with Bob's daughter, Elise, and I knew he still held some kind of grudge against me because Elise had now left town. "You've done all right for yourself, haven't you?"

I bit back a swear word and said, "I'd get rid of it in an instant if it meant bringing Bob back."

Zen walked into the lounge, hissed at Lester, and bristled up his tail. Even Zen was a good judge of character.

"Get that thing away from me," Lester snarled at Zen.

"The cat stays." I rested a hand on my hip and tilted my head. "Now, do you want to sit?" I indicated the sofa. He was just about to sit down when Zen beat him to it and jumped up onto one of the cushions. He sized Lester up, eyes half-closed, wiggling his rear end like he was about to pounce.

"Er...no, I think I'll stand." Lester eyed Zen warily and took a step toward the window.

I sat, curled up my legs, and stroked Zen's chin.

Lester looked out of the window, his back to me. "Did you see anyone else hanging around Pandora's house when you arrived?"

"No, just Tim Baxtor. Do you think someone could've sneaked in the back patio door?"

He swung around and folded his arms across his chest. "*I'm* asking the questions here." He paused for a moment. "Do you think someone could've sneaked in the back patio door?" he asked me as if he'd suddenly thought of it himself.

I looked at him for a few seconds. Did an inward sigh before answering. "Yes, it's possible. I heard that Tim said he was framed."

"Where did you hear that?" he snapped. "That's not common knowledge. We haven't released a statement yet."

Oops! I wasn't about to expose Vernon or his contact. If in doubt, change the subject. "Er..." I waved a hand vaguely in the air. "What about Ian, Pandora's son? Do you think he could be involved?"

"Highly unlikely."

"Does he have an alibi? If he inherited Pandora's estate, that would also be a motive."

"What, like you inheriting Bob's estate?"

I thought back to how Lester had tried to pin Bob's murder on me for the very same reason. And how annoyed he was to be proved wrong.

Zen growled at Lester.

Good boy!

"But he's a doctor. He'd have had access to the pentobarbital that killed Pandora, too."

"Are you telling me how to do my job?"

Yes? "Um...no."

"Good.

"What about you?" Lester asked me.

"What about me?"

"Maybe you had a motive."

"I'd never met her before!"

"It's just that people who come into contact with you have a habit of dying."

"No way. Don't even think about trying to blame me for this. We had an appointment with Pandora."

"Tell me again exactly how long it was between seeing Tim Baxtor leave the house and finding Pandora dead."

"About five minutes."

Lester wrote that down on a pad he pulled from his pocket and underlined it several times with large slashes across the page. "Did you see Tim carrying anything when he left? Like a pair of gloves?"

"No, I didn't notice anything in his hands, but I guess they could've been in his pockets. He had dress trousers on."

He paced up and down in front of the window for a while, then turned to me. "I think it's pretty obvious what happened."

"Really?" It wasn't to me. It was far from obvious.

"Yes." Lester gave me a smug smile. "Tim called himself on a disposable cell and fabricated the story that Pandora called him saying she had evidence about what had really happened to Jenna. I think he went to her house with the express intention of killing Pandora."

I frowned. That didn't make sense either. The timing of it all was strange. "But why kill her after all these years though? It doesn't fit."

He gave a nonchalant shrug. "It's just a question of making it fit."

CHAPTER SEVEN

If Lester Marshall wasn't going to investigate any other possibilities, then it was up to us to discover the truth. And I had an idea of how to find out more about this drug that had killed Pandora. I called my vet's office and booked an appointment for later in the morning to take Karma for his last inoculation.

Zen and Karma sat at my feet, watching me as I made the call. Zen looked at Karma with an *uh-oh!* look on his face. I swear Zen was a human in a past life.

I channeled some positive energy after Lester's visit, with a revitalizing flow of sun salutations, followed by meditation, green tea, and what Tara would call rabbit food. I was just rebraiding the front of my hair to keep it out of my eyes when my cell rang.

"Morning," Harvey said. "How's things?"

My heart did a little triple loop at his voice. "Good, thanks. Where are you?" I felt a pang of longing.

"Still in Seattle, I'm afraid. I stayed overnight at the apartment of one of the guys from the uni. It's taking longer than I thought to catalogue everything I've recovered. Hopefully, I'll be back later today though. I'll pop into the tavern. Have you found out any more about Pandora?"

"A little." I told him what had happened so far.

"Please be careful. If Tim didn't murder Pandora, then there's still a dangerous killer on the loose, and I don't want anything to happen to you. It was bad enough last time."

I thought back to that night when both of us came so close to dying after we'd discovered who'd murdered Bob. It wasn't exactly on my bucket list to repeat, either. "I will—don't worry."

Three hours later, I was in Adam Whitaker's office at the Danger Cove Vet Clinic. Every time I'd been to see him before he'd been very quiet and reserved, and I didn't know how easy it was going to be to get any useful information out of him. He wasn't unfriendly, exactly. I just think he preferred talking to animals rather than humans. Half the time I didn't blame him. I could totally relate to that.

"And how are you today, Karma?" Adam opened Karma's travel cage and lifted out my three-legged friend, putting him on the treatment table..

"I'm fine!" I squeaked in my best kitten impression. "I'm just here for my nasty little injection. Please be gentle with me."

Adam gave me an odd look. What? Was it just me who put voices in my cats' mouths? But seriously, why ask Karma how he was if you didn't expect an answer?

I coughed. "Er...he's fine. Just needs his final jab."

Adam read Karma's notes while stroking the length of his body. Then he nodded, opened a drawer, and pulled out a prefilled syringe.

I held on to Karma and gave him a reassuring scratch around the ears while Adam got ready. It was quickly administered, and Karma was licking his hand.

"All done." Adam wrote on an inoculations card for me and handed it over.

"Great. Um...I wanted to ask you a couple of questions, actually, while I'm here. It's about the drug pentobarbital. I understand it can be used to euthanize animals and prevent seizures."

He blinked rapidly. "Do you think Karma has had a seizure?"

"No."

"Well, it's not our policy to euthanize healthy animals. If you need to rehome him, we can put up a notice in the waiting room. Or you could take him to the Second Chance animal shelter." A look of disgust crossed his face.

"Oh, no, it's nothing like that. I'm keeping Karma." I stroked him more vigorously—Karma, not Adam—just in case he knew what we were talking about, like Zen always seemed to. I'd been racking my brain trying to decide how to broach the subject and decided that honesty was the best policy. Lying to people didn't sit comfortably with me, and I was already in deep karma doo-doo from the huge amount of lies I'd told during my last investigation. In my defense, I had been trying to save myself from being wrongfully accused of murder, but still, I didn't need any more, thanks. "I don't know if you heard about Pandora's death?"

He frowned. "No. I don't think we have a patient called Pandora. What kind of animal was she?"

"Pandora Williams," I said. "She lived in town. She did holistic therapies from her home. She was murdered with pentobarbital."

"How awful." He blinked rapidly this time, his face turning pale. "I didn't know her, I'm afraid."

"I was wondering how long it would take to work," I said.

"To kill someone?" His eyes nearly bugged out of their sockets.

"Yes."

"Well, that depends on how it's administered and in what dose. It comes in tablet and liquid form. Tablets would take longer to work. With animals it's given intravenously and euthanizes them in seconds. It would be the same for humans, given the right dose."

"Right." My brain cells fired up, mind replaying the scene. Pandora was already dead when we'd arrived after seeing Tim hurrying out of the house. Despite my initial reservations, he had to have been the one to kill her. I doubted there was enough time for someone else to sneak in the rear door after Tim left, give her a shot, and then leave in the time it took Ruby and me to get inside. Was there?

"It's worrying that you should mention pentobarbital though." Adam's voice interrupted my thoughts. "We had a break-in here a couple of weeks ago, and some of it was stolen."

"Really?"

"Yes. One vial was taken. I reported it to the police, and they sent out some crime scene people to check for fingerprints."

"Did they find any?

"They did, but apparently they weren't a match to anyone in their database. And no witnesses came forward, so they have no viable leads or suspects. It happened in the early hours of the morning."

"How did they get into the building?"

"A window was smashed in the bathroom, and they crawled through."

"Do you have any CCTV cameras?"

"We didn't think we needed to in a town like this. We've installed them now, of course. The alarm system was very old and had apparently developed some kind of fault we didn't know about. We've updated that too. Gosh, I hope it wasn't *our* pentobarbital that resulted in Pandora's death!"

CHAPTER EIGHT

———

I finished fixing a champagne cocktail for a couple who were traveling around the state on their honeymoon. They'd just been out snorkeling around the rocks at Two Mile Beach and enthusiastically told me about every fish they'd spotted. I poured their drinks and added a maraschino cherry and a slice of orange peel to the edge of the glasses, thinking that my Smugglers' coladas would definitely be off the menu for the foreseeable future. All I could see when I thought about them was the glass in front of Pandora's lifeless body and the empty bottle of white rum on the table.

My cell rang as the couple drifted away to a booth. It was Harvey.

"Hey!" I said. "What are you up to?"

"I'm up to my eyes in paperwork and bones and gold coins. I love the hands-on stuff of my job. When you get to recover ancient artifacts—things that no one else has clapped eyes on for centuries—it's mind blowing. But then all the paperwork involved in cataloguing everything does my head in!"

"Hmmm…I didn't know eyes could clap." I chuckled. I was still getting my head around some of Harvey's Brit-speak.

He laughed back, warm and throaty. I felt a stirring deep inside.

"Will you be back later?"

"No, I'm afraid not. That's why I'm giving you a bell now. You know I said my boss thought he could spare some help from the museum? Well, a colleague is on their way right now. I'm picking them up from the airport tonight, so I won't get time to see you, I don't think."

A twinge of disappointment kicked in, but at least this was good news. Hopefully, if he had more help, it meant Harvey

and I would get to spend some more quality time together.
"That's fantastic." My mind wandered to what we could start
doing with said quality time. Breakfast in bed. A romantic walk
along the beach, stargazing. Snuggled up together on the sofa
watching a movie.

"Yes," Harvey said, although there was something in his
voice that sounded a little off. "I'm so knackered at the moment,
I could do with a night in front of the box, snuggled up with you,
but looks like that won't happen tonight."

"Box? What box?"

"The telly."

"Huh? You've totally lost me now."

"The TV!" He laughed again. "Anyway, better go. See
ya later."

As I was hanging up, Vernon walked in to start his shift.
I grabbed him and pulled him behind the bar. Ruby took a food
order out to the pub garden and then joined us. I told them what
Adam had said.

"What if Tim didn't kill Pandora, and he really was set
up?" I said. "It can't just be a coincidence that someone broke
into the vet's and stole the same drug used to kill her. Tim
wouldn't have needed to *steal* it when he had access to it at his
pharmacy."

"Maybe Tim stole it to throw suspicion on someone
else," Vernon said.

"Yeah, I suppose that's possible," I agreed. "But then Ian
could've also done the same thing."

"What about Tim's wife, Donna?" Vernon asked. "She
could be a suspect. Maybe she had some kind of grudge against
Pandora, especially if she'd been bad-mouthing her husband.
What do you know about her?" he asked Ruby.

"Donna was born in Danger Cove, and when Tim was
studying to be a pharmacist at the university, Donna was on the
same course, so I guess they knew each other there. Tim started
going out with her about five years after Jenna disappeared.
Then they got married, and they now work together in the store.
Pandora told me she was devastated that Tim was happily
married, getting on with his life as if nothing had happened. I
think she probably hated Donna as much as Tim. She couldn't

understand why someone would marry him after he'd been so obviously linked to Jenna's disappearance."

"But he was cleared of any involvement at the time," Vernon said.

"Yes, but mud sticks, doesn't it?"

"There's no accounting for true love, though. It makes you oblivious to everything else," Vernon said, avoiding Ruby's gaze.

"I've only met Donna around town a few times, just to say hello to in passing," Ruby added. "I don't really know much about her, but I can't imagine she'd be too happy if Pandora was about to start publicly accusing Tim again. It would affect their business, wouldn't it?"

Vernon rubbed his stomach, his face scrunching up as if he was in pain.

"What?" Ruby glanced at him. "Are you okay?"

"Yeah, yeah. I'm fine." He stopped rubbing.

"You don't look fine, actually. You've gone all pale."

"Maybe you're overdoing things, working here," I suggested.

"I'm sixty-two, not a hundred and two. There's still plenty of life left in me. I'm fine." Vernon wiped a few beads of sweat away from his forehead. "Anyway, what were we saying?"

I eyed him carefully. He still looked pale, but Vernon wasn't the type who liked sympathy or being babied. He made a hand gesture for me to carry on and perched on the edge of a barstool.

"If Tim wanted to make it look like someone else, he wouldn't have gone to her house in daylight to do it when there was a risk of being seen," I said.

"Don't forget the phone call," Vernon said. "Tim claims Pandora called him and wanted to talk to him about finding some evidence about Jenna's disappearance. That's the reason he said he was there."

"But then when he got there, he could've seen the perfect opportunity and killed her," Ruby said.

"If she called him, where's the cell phone?" I asked. "The police said she didn't have one."

"Anyone can get hold of a disposable phone," Vernon said. "My contact said the police searched the house but didn't find one. And Lester Marshall's in charge—don't forget, and he's a few fries short of a Happy Meal."

I nodded my agreement. "Remember when he was investigating Bob's murder and he got the crime scene people to search Bob's office for evidence but not his apartment, and we had to do it ourselves? They probably didn't look hard enough."

"He gets fixated on who he thinks the suspect is and only does half a job," Vernon said. "Maybe the phone call is the key to this. We need to get into Pandora's house and have a good look around. Not just for the phone, but if Pandora really did make that call, then we might find some kind of 'evidence' that Jenna is still alive."

"And if she didn't make the call? How does that fit?" I said. "It would mean Tim just happened to go to her house at a time when she was drunk, with a lethal dose of pentobarbital already in his pocket, and that sounds too opportunistic to me. There are so many flaws with that plan. You said yourself Pandora hated Tim. She wouldn't have just opened the door to him, would she, unless they had some kind of prior arrangement?"

Ruby chewed on her crimson-painted lip, pondering that. "No, I'm pretty sure she wouldn't have."

"So Pandora must've called him," Vernon said.

"Or maybe someone else had been watching her, stalking her, waiting for an opportunity," I said, thinking back to her rear garden. "If you were standing on the other side of her fence in the woods, you could probably look into her kitchen window. Maybe the killer saw her slumped at the kitchen table in a drunken sleep. Because I still don't know why Tim would do it now, after all this time, unless she really did call him and say she had some kind of evidence about Jenna."

"Yes, but maybe this evidence might've been something she found out that proved Tim had murdered Jenna all those years ago. He'd definitely want to shut her up then, wouldn't he?"

"That makes sense." Ruby nodded vigorously.

Vernon scrunched up his face, thinking. "But why do it in broad daylight with a chance of being spotted? *If* Pandora called him and said she had such evidence that was going to put him away, why not arrange to go to her house when it was dark? Or meet somewhere secluded? And why didn't he leave through the back door and over the fence, disappearing into the woods, where there was less chance of being spotted? Why go straight out the front door where people could see?"

"Maybe he panicked," Ruby said. "It must be pretty stressful murdering someone. Perhaps he wasn't thinking straight. Don't they always say there's no such thing as a perfect murder?"

"That's possible, but Tim must be a reasonably intelligent guy if he's a pharmacist. I can't believe he wouldn't have gone out the back," Vernon said.

"There are too many questions," I said.

"Exactly. That's why we need to get inside and have a good look around to see if Lester and Co. missed anything." Vernon nodded. "Tonight. We'll go there when it's dark. I can get us inside with no problems."

"Break in, you mean?" Ruby whispered, eyes rounding.

"Er...excuse me. I'm looking for Ruby Fournier?" A male voice interrupted our hushed conversation.

I glanced over at the bar. A tall, skinny guy with strawberry-blond hair and freckles stood there. Even from this distance I could smell disinfectant and that horrible scent that hits your nostrils when you go inside a hospital. I didn't need to be psychic to work out who this was.

"Yes, I'm Ruby." She gave him her hand and a warm smile. "You must be Ian?"

"Yes." He nodded grimly, shaking her hand.

She placed her other hand on top of his. "My condolences. I'm so sorry for your loss."

"Thank you. Is there somewhere we could talk?"

"Of course." Ruby rounded the bar and took hold of his elbow, leading him outside into the garden, which was now quiet. Before she walked out the front door, she glanced over her shoulder and beckoned me to follow.

By the time I got outside, they'd chosen a secluded corner table. "Hi, I'm Hope Foster." I offered my hand, and he shook it with a firm but cold grasp. "I'm really sorry about your mom."

He nodded at me.

"Can I get you something to drink?"

"No, I'm fine, thanks." He turned to Ruby as I sat down next to her. "Thank you for calling me. I don't even know where to begin with the funeral arrangements. I don't know who to invite to her wake. Don't know who her friends were anymore. I was hoping someone who knew her could help me out. I...haven't seen Mother in a long time. I mean, *hadn't* seen her."

Ruby reached out and patted his hand. "I understand. She told me how difficult things were after Jenna."

Ian looked away, out over the cliffs toward the lighthouse.

"It's tragic what happened to your mom and sister," I said.

"Jenna. Yes." Ian gave a small, almost imperceptible shake of his head and avoided our eyes, as if the memories were too painful. Eventually he turned back to us. "I've just been at the police station. They think Tim murdered Mother. They think she'd found some kind of evidence finally that he'd killed Jenna, and confronted him about it."

"That's the way it looks," Ruby said.

"Did they tell you they'd found anything when they searched her house?" I asked Ian.

"No. They said they didn't find anything that might help them. My sister was six years older than me." He placed his neat, manicured fingers on the table and stared at them. "Twenty-three when she just disappeared. I'm sure you know the story?"

"I do," Ruby said.

"Both Mother and I always thought Tim had killed her. Mother almost lost her mind afterward. Had a breakdown. She wanted to get revenge on Tim, so she did everything she could to disrupt his life. Cause problems with his business. Ruin his reputation."

"I heard he threatened her with lawsuits, and she was arrested," I said.

"Yes." Ian sighed. "I told her it had to stop. I loved my sister. We were a close family at one time, but all that just fell apart. I knew Jenna wouldn't have left without saying good-bye. Everyone knew it. We just couldn't prove it. But Mother wouldn't let it go. She became depressed. She didn't have any time for me. She could barely talk to me sometimes, let alone look at me. I think I reminded her of Jenna. Of what she'd lost, you know? I was the one left, and she didn't want me there. She wanted Jenna. I felt guilty, most of the time, that I was still alive."

I felt his grief palpably in the air. What an impossibly awful situation.

"So we drifted apart. I left to go to the university, and I never came back. I got a job in Seattle and stayed there."

"And you're a cardiologist?" I asked, catching Ruby's eye. A cardiologist with access to pentobarbital. Could Ian be the murderer? Could he have framed Tim?

"Yes."

"So you hadn't visited your mom in a long time?" I asked.

He ran a hand through his hair and shifted in his seat as if he was uncomfortable. "No. We were estranged. That's why I don't know who to contact about her funeral. But you knew her." He looked at Ruby. "Can you tell me how she was these last few years?"

"I only met her about ten years ago when she restarted up her healing therapies. She told me about you and Jenna, of course. And how she'd had a breakdown and become a recluse. She was still a recluse when I knew her, only leaving the house for essentials. She didn't have many friends, and only really saw people when they went to her house for treatments. In spite of everything she'd been through, she still wanted to help others, but I guess she just didn't have the strength to help herself."

"So things didn't change much?" Ian said.

"I think she was still very sad about Jenna after all this time. I used to pop in to see her sometimes when I didn't have a treatment scheduled. Just to make sure she was okay. I wanted to look out for her. Let her know she wasn't alone. I invited her for days out with me, just to get her away from the house. A change of scenery can do so much good. But she always refused.

Although she didn't admit it, I think she didn't want to leave in case Jenna did come back and she wasn't there."

"That sounds about right." Ian nodded solemnly. "Do you really think she found something to prove he killed Jenna?"

"I don't know," I said.

"There still isn't a day that goes by when I don't wonder if Jenna could be out there somewhere. I need to get an answer. I need some kind of closure. To find out once and for all. But Tim is denying any part in Jenna's or Mother's death, and I don't know what to do. You knew Mother," he said to Ruby. "Will you help me try to find out if she discovered something about Jenna before she was killed?"

"Of course we will," Ruby said.

"Do you have the keys to Pandora's house? We should start there and see if the police missed something. Lester Marshall isn't exactly renowned for his thorough investigation skills." I hadn't been thrilled at the thought of breaking and entering, and now, hopefully, we wouldn't have to.

"Yes, the police gave them to me. They said they'd finished examining it, and...well, everything Mother left is mine now, so we're entitled to take a look." A hand went to his pocket, and he patted the keys with a jangling sound.

CHAPTER NINE

———

Ian left his red Range Rover with the vanity plate of *Cardio1* in the tavern's parking lot, and we went in Vernon's car, while Ruby stayed to man (or, rather woman) the tavern. A chill crept through me as Vernon parked outside Pandora's house. I pictured everything as it had been when we'd discovered her body: Tim rushing out and up the path, that crazed look in his eye, as if he'd seen a ghost.

I glanced around the quiet street. Opposite Pandora's house an elderly man was in his front garden, tending to a healthy rose bush. Further along, a mom pushed a buggy, the child inside swinging her legs and licking an ice cream cone. Granted, it was only just after 1:00 p.m., and we'd arrived at four the last time, but it was still a street full of families and retirees, so someone would usually be around. Why risk going out the front door where the chance of being spotted was so high, when he could've left from the rear and become invisible? I knew Ruby was convinced of Tim's involvement, but it was bugging me. Surely a guilty person wouldn't leave through the front exit.

I took a deep breath and followed Vernon and Ian to the front door. Ian unlocked it, swinging it open, and stood frozen on the step, glancing down the hallway, up the stairs.

"It's so strange coming back here. Brings back a lot of memories."

"It's bound to." I placed a hand on his back and patted. "Take your time."

He inhaled a lungful of air. Held it. Then blew it out forcefully before taking a step over the threshold. He glanced around again. "I don't know where to start. Don't know what I'm looking for. What could Mother have possibly found that would prove Tim Baxtor killed Jenna?"

I didn't have a clue either, but I guessed it would be glaringly obvious when we found it. If we found it.

"We need to take it room by room to be thorough," Vernon said. "I'll take the dining room. You guys start with the lounge."

Ian and I walked into the lounge.

His gaze hit the photos of a beautiful young woman. "Jenna." He stopped suddenly, his hand reaching for his heart, before moving toward them.

They were everywhere. On the mantel above the fireplace, on top of the old-fashioned box TV, on a battered chest of drawers underneath the window, the glass coffee table. Jenna stared back at us at various ages. With a much-younger Pandora, Jenna sitting on her knee, a pink bow in her hair, eyes sparkling, little cherub cheeks pink. Sitting on a swing in a park, her long hair trailing behind her as she swung high in the air with a gap-toothed smile. At her high school graduation, clutching a certificate, with a proud-looking Pandora beaming at her daughter. On the beach as a teenager, sand covering her hands and face as she built a sand castle, a bucket and shovel lying next to her.

There were no photos of Ian anywhere, and my heart ached for him. It was hard enough losing a sister and never knowing what happened to her. But in the aftermath, Ian and Pandora had lost each other too.

Ian picked up the photo of Jenna, petite and fragile looking, at her graduation, his finger gently caressing the glass. I turned away to allow him some private reflection and opened one of the drawers in the chest, unsure what we were really looking for, while Vernon checked the dining room opposite from us. It didn't seem likely Jenna was still alive, but if she was, and if Pandora had found proof, what could that be? A letter from her daughter? A passport or driver's license application? Had Bud Ohlsen checked Jenna's bank accounts when she'd disappeared, to see if there'd been any activity? I wondered if her account had been closed years ago or whether it was kept open to monitor any deposits or withdrawals.

I found numerous wallet-style folders and pulled out a pile of papers from the first one. They were all charcoal sketches of various scenic spots around Danger Cove. The lighthouse, the harbor, the vintage tourist trolley that traveled on a loop between Main Street and the pier, a tide pool on the beach, then Pandora's portrait, and Ian posing with a fishing rod in hand as a little boy, one foot on a jagged rock.

Ian appeared at my shoulder, taking them from me and shuffling through. He sat down on the sagging sofa with a heavy slump. "These were Jenna's. She was so talented. Always sketching something. She'd just been offered a job with a prestigious design company in Seattle, when she went missing."

"Is that why Jenna wanted to break up with Tim? Because he didn't want her to take the job?"

He stared up at the ceiling. "Jenna didn't tell me about the specifics of her relationship with Tim. She was kind of a private person, and I guess she thought her little brother wouldn't understand anyway. When they first met, she seemed really happy. She told me she was in love with him, but...I don't know. He was her first real relationship. I think she just got too caught up in things too early.

"As the years went on, I noticed a change in her. She used to wear such bright and colorful clothes. She was an artist, after all, and expressed herself and her moods in the things she wore. Gradually, she started toning down the colors, wearing more black and gray. The skirts got longer, the tops less revealing. She wore less makeup. Lost touch with her friends. She'd had a best friend since kindergarten, Melanie Crook, and she used to hang out with her all the time before Tim. Then it got so she'd make excuses to not see Melanie, and she spent all her time with Tim. I don't think he liked it if she was out of his sight. In the last few months before she disappeared, whenever she was at home, she was moody and withdrawn. Something was on her mind. I'm sure. Something that was worrying her. She was probably working out how to break it off with Tim without causing too many problems."

"Was Tim ever violent toward her?"

"I don't think so. I never saw any bruises or anything. But I think he was jealous and controlling, and that's why she was going to break up with him that night. And yes, I don't think Tim wanted her to take that job in Seattle."

"Do you think she was afraid of him?"

"I doubt it. Not seriously, anyway, otherwise she wouldn't have gone to meet him that night alone, would she?" He closed his eyes briefly. When he opened them, they were glistening with unshed tears. "But it's easy to underestimate people. She should've been afraid. Even though we could never prove it, I'm sure he killed her. He couldn't stand the fact that she was leaving him, and probably lost his temper and somehow got rid of her body with no one ever finding it."

He continued looking through the sketches, a tear visibly snaking down his cheek. I left him to his grief and searched the rest of the drawers. I found a box file and pulled it out, sitting and resting it on my lap as I flicked through financial papers inside.

According to Pandora's checking account statements, she made very few withdrawals and lived frugally, which I guessed was how you'd expect a recluse to live. It looked as if she hadn't updated her furniture or home with modern items, and if she hardly went out of the house, then I couldn't imagine her doing much shopping. There were also statements from her savings accounts, and I calculated that she had around two million dollars when she died. Underneath Pandora's accounts were some old-looking bank statements, yellowed with age, the print from an old dot-matrix printer faded. The name on the account was Jenna Williams. The last statement was dated two years after she'd disappeared. Attached to it was a letter from the bank saying the account had been closed. Well, that answered one of my questions.

I flicked back through them, searching for evidence of withdrawals or deposits after July 4 twenty years ago, but there were none. Wherever Jenna had gone, she hadn't used her bank account. And she hadn't withdrawn any significant amounts of money from it prior to disappearing. After putting them back, I looked in the last drawer but found nothing that could be a clue. I closed it, and Ian put the sketches back into the folder.

"I haven't found anything yet that might help us," I said.

"Neither have I," Vernon called out from the dining room.

We headed for the kitchen. I was half expecting Pandora's body to still be as we'd found it the other day. But, of course, that was ridiculous. The chair she'd been sitting on was still lying on the floor. The glasses had been removed, along with the bottle of rum, the syringe wrapper, and the vial.

Ian glanced around the room. "Everything is just the same as when I left. It's like stepping into a time warp." He pinched the bridge of his nose, as if trying to hold back more tears.

It was true. The countertops were chipped and peeling, the freestanding stove looked as if it was on its last legs.

Pandora's purse hung from a hook behind the door. Ian went through it, finding her wallet, complete with a hundred and fifty-two dollars inside, a credit card, a packet of tissues, a comb, a slim book on crystals, and a few loose toothpicks. At least if her wallet was still here, it could definitely rule out a burglary of any kind as a motive for her murder. And I very much doubted a thief would've wanted to steal the old TV. Nothing seemed to have been searched or rifled through by a thief, either.

As Ian and Vernon searched closets, I opened a drawer of cutlery, but there was nothing of interest. The next drawer down held some dishcloths, a diary, and an address book. I flicked through the address book, but nothing was marked on any of the pages. I put it back and called out to them. "I found a diary here." It was small and cheap and didn't look well used.

Ian and Vernon stood beside me as I went through every page. No entries. Nothing to say she'd arranged to meet Tim on that fateful day.

"There's a calendar." Vernon pointed to a hook on the wall next to the ancient fridge and removed it, placing it on the counter. It was long and narrow, with a picture of a tropical beach at the top of the page. There were several things written on it.

Ian ran his finger down the page. "Two weeks ago she had an appointment with a Dr. Trower." He scrunched his face up, thinking. "Trower. That sounds familiar, but I can't place it. Is he a GP here?"

"No," Vernon said. "I don't think he's local to Danger Cove. I've never heard of him."

"Tania Fuller—2:00 p.m." Ian tapped another entry a couple of days before Pandora's death. "Do you know her?"

I nodded. "She works in Veggie Tables." I pointed to some more entries. "Look, there she is, once a week. She obviously had a regular appointment with Pandora for Reiki treatment."

He pointed to the only entry listed for the day Pandora was killed. "Yours and Ruby's names are here but nothing listed for Tim."

"Yes, Ruby phoned her in the morning, and she said we could come over the same day."

Ian flicked back a month. Tania's name regularly appeared, along with some other names.

"Looks like they're all clients too." I pointed to other names with a single note next to them about which kind of treatment they were booked for.

"And another appointment with Dr. Trower." Ian laid the diary on the counter. He slumped down at one of the chairs. "Was Mother ill?"

"I don't know," I said. "I never met her before that day, but Ruby didn't mention anything like that, so she obviously hadn't said anything to her if she was."

Ian's eyes glistened again. "I never got to say good-bye to her. I should've tried harder to get our relationship on track." He flopped his head into his hands. "And now it's too late."

I reached out and gently squeezed his shoulder. My heart welled up inside.

"Let's look upstairs," Vernon suggested.

"I don't want to go into Jenna's room," Ian said. "Mother always left it exactly how it was when Jenna died, and I don't think I can face that as well. I'll search my old room."

Vernon took Pandora's room and the bathroom. When I stepped into Jenna's, it was like stepping back into the mid-90s. The place was a shrine to Jenna's memory. There was an empty, hollow feel in the room, and it smelled musty. A single wrought iron bed sat underneath the dormer window, a clean white duvet on top. The headboard had ornamental poles at either end, and looped around one were various beaded bracelets in different colors. A selection of reproduction prints hung on the walls. I didn't know much about the classic painters, but I recognized an Andy Warhol and a Picasso. There were also several more sketches in frames up there. I inspected them closer and saw Jenna's now familiar signature in the bottom corner. There was a large stereo on the edge of a white dressing table. I flicked through a pile of CDs stacked at the side of it. Simply Red, Celine Dion, Michael Jackson, Mariah Carey. I could picture Jenna propped up on her bed all those years ago, listening to music, sketching away, her long hair fanning across the pillow.

There was a bright-blue jewelry box on top of the table. I opened it and found tangles of silver and beads: an amethyst crystal bracelet, one made of hematite, a big lump of rose quartz, a silver bracelet with charms of feathers attached, dangly earrings.

Next, I tackled the drawers in the dressing table, but there was nothing much there except more costume jewelry, hair products, makeup, all crusty and congealed. I worked my way through the wardrobe, running a hand along the clothes—dresses, jeans, T-shirts that had been hanging in the same spot for twenty years, gathering dust, waiting for Jenna's hopeful return. There were a couple of cardboard shoe boxes on the top shelf, which I rifled through, but they only contained a pair of cork wedged heels, a pair of boots, and several pairs of flip-flops, nothing that showed Jenna was alive and well today.

We finally gave up, and on the way out we passed Pandora's mailbox. I opened it up and pulled out a pile of letters, handing them to Ian. "Do you want to check through these?" If Pandora had received a letter from Jenna, maybe there was another one in here.

"Can you do it? I need to get out of here. I need some time to get my head round things."

"Of course," I said.

"Are you staying here while you're in town?" Vernon asked.

"I...I hadn't thought about it. I guess so, for a few days maybe. But right at this minute I need to be alone. Can you drop me off at Two Mile Beach? I need to walk."

"Sure," Vernon said.

We drove in silence, each of us lost in our own thoughts. When Vernon and I returned to the tavern, the place was heaving, so it wasn't until nearly 10:00 p.m. when I got a chance to go through Pandora's mail. I sat at the bar and opened the first envelope. It was an invitation to a holistic healing exhibition in Seattle. The next one was a generic letter from her bank, inquiring if she wanted a loan. The last one was on letter-headed white paper from Seattle General Hospital, confirming an appointment with Dr. Trower the following month, and letting Pandora know the results of some recent tests she'd had.

"Guys, look at this." I waved Ruby and Vernon over. "Dr. Trower is an oncology consultant." I handed Ruby the letter and watched her face droop as she read.

Vernon studied it over her shoulder. "So Pandora had a brain tumor? And judging by these test results, it was inoperable. I wonder how long she had left."

"Not long enough, thanks to Tim Baxtor," Ruby muttered.

CHAPTER TEN

I woke early the next morning, made a chamomile tea, and stood in front of the large windows in my lounge, staring out at the breathtaking scenery, mulling over Pandora's death and Jenna's disappearance. What had happened to the whole family as a result of Jenna's disappearance had started a chain reaction of tragedy. And it looked like Ian still wouldn't find any long-awaited answers. Had Pandora really found something that would connect Tim to killing Jenna all those years ago? If so, what could that possibly have been? Whatever it was, it looked like those answers went to her grave with her.

I glanced down onto the pub garden and cliffs, noticing Harvey arriving with more equipment. Someone else was with him. She had straight blonde hair hanging down to her narrow waist, a heart-shaped face, and pouty lips. She wore denim cutoff shorts that revealed long, slim legs, along with plenty of cheek, and a T-shirt with the word *Whatever* written across her ample chest. It was so tight it looked like it could cut off her circulation, and so low that the whole neighborhood would be treated to a free lacey bra-cup show. With the amount of makeup she had on, it looked as if she was going to a nightclub.

So this was the help that Portsmouth Naval Museum had sent over to assist him with his find?

A prickle of jealousy flared inside, and I tried to push it away. So what if she was gorgeous? Harvey and I were together now. And yes, even though we'd both been too busy to spend much time with each other lately, things were fantastic between us.

I watched as they chatted. He bent down to put the equipment on the ground outside the privacy tent. She bent next to him, leaning in close to his ear. She put a hand on his arm, saying something I couldn't hear. Then she rubbed that hand up his arm toward his shoulder, his neck, and ruffled the hair at his nape.

Hey! Stop touching him!

Hopefully, I was hallucinating. I blinked several times, but she was still there. As she ran her fingertips toward his chest, I leaned closer to the window to get a better look and banged my forehead.

Ouch!

I stepped back, rubbing my forehead, then put my tea down and hurriedly dressed in some harem pants and a peach off-the-shoulder peasant top. Zen and Karma were waiting at the door to be let out for their morning duties, and they shot through as soon as I opened it. I'd installed a cat door when I'd moved in, but most of the time they still wanted me to open the people door for them.

The wind was fresh, and I rubbed my arms as I rounded the outside of the tavern to approach Harvey and Blondie. When I reached them, she was laughing about something as she picked up a tool belt laden with small trowels and paintbrushes. She looked like she was on a modeling shoot for a guy's magazine, not about to begin an archeological dig.

She clipped it around her tiny waist and then said to Harvey, "I've forgotten how good we were together. I've missed you." She reached out and rested the palm of her hand on his cheek.

Before Harvey could say anything, I announced my presence with an overenthusiastic "Hi!" to mask the disappointment that had just slammed into my ribs. Was she an ex-girlfriend of his?

Harvey jumped away from her.

Blondie looked me up and down with that unmistakable curled lip of a jealous female, visually assessing me with a haughty glare and obviously finding me lacking.

"Hi!" Harvey stood and put his arm around me, kissing my cheek.

Blondie's eyes narrowed slightly at the gesture.

"This is Carmen." Harvey swung his arm in Blondie's direction. "She's come to help with the salvage. This is Hope."

"Nice to meet you," I said.

Her eyes brightened up then when Harvey looked at her. "Lovely to meet you too, Holly," she said with a British accent, giving me a smile that was obviously fake.

I wrapped my arm tighter round Harvey's waist. "It's Hope, actually."

She ignored my comment. "Yes, Harvey and I are going to be working closely together now to recover the rest of the artifacts he found." She looked pretty smug about that.

Was it me, or did she just emphasize the word *closely*?

"How...nice," I said, forcing the smile to stay on my face. "Any news on the *Ocean's Revenge*?" I asked Harvey.

"Now that Carmen's here to help, I'll be going back out again with the crew from the Seattle research department at Uni of Washington to look for it. We've marked out a bigger search area this time. I'm pretty confident we'll find it soon. But how about you? What have you been doing?"

Carmen climbed down into the entrance to the caves and left us alone, so I filled him in on what we'd discovered about Pandora.

"Crikey." He ran a hand through his messy crop, and I wanted to do the same. "Must be awful for Ian."

"Yeah, I feel really sorry for him, but I can't help thinking he may have something to do with Pandora's death. Even so, I still want to try to help him find some closure about Jenna."

"But the police are pretty sure that Tim's the one who killed Pandora?"

"Looks that way. Maybe they're right. But something is still niggling at me."

"Anyway, I'm sorry, but I can't stop. I'm meeting the crew at the harbor. I'll drop by tonight when I'm done for the day."

"Okay." I leaned in to kiss his warm lips, then stood watching his retreating back, admiring the view, when Carmen climbed out of the entrance.

"You know, we went out with each other for ages," she said to me, not even bothering with the fake smile now that Harvey wasn't in the vicinity. "And I can tell you with absolute certainty. You're definitely not his type." She gave me the once-over again.

Zen chose that moment to stalk up behind us. He swiped the back of Carmen's leg with his paw, scratching her.

"Bloody hell!" She leaped into the air with a surprised yell. Looked at her leg. Looked at Zen. Then tried to kick him.

Zen was too fast for her and ran off. I swear I heard him snigger.

CHAPTER ELEVEN

———

My head whirled as I refilled salt and pepper shakers at the bar, although I actually spilled more than I put in because I was too busy thinking about Carmen and Harvey. Was it true? Was she really Harvey's ex? Why did Harvey keep the fact she was coming out here to help him from me? That twinge of jealousy turned into a full-blown sucker punch to my stomach, because judging by what I'd seen earlier, Carmen wasn't too bothered about the *ex* word. It seemed like she wanted Harvey back. But I'd been there before. My previous fiancé had cheated on me, which was why I'd invented the no-dating rule. I hadn't been involved with a guy for years. Hadn't even wanted to until Harvey appeared in my life. And I didn't want to be a green-eyed monster either. Ruby had once told me that worrying about bad stuff that might happen was like praying for what you don't want. And I agreed. Although it was hard to follow that advice when my heart was twisting. Even though I'd only known Harvey a short time, there was a connection there that I knew was something special. Maybe even once-in-a-lifetime special. And I didn't relish the idea of Carmen waltzing in and trying to cause trouble between us. I knew her type. She was exactly the same as Elise.

Ruby breezed through the door of the tavern an hour before her shift was due to start, which was a welcome distraction from my worrying. "Morning, darling!"

"Morning." I tried to sound like my usual happy self, but my voice wobbled a bit.

"Oh, what's wrong?" Ruby frowned. "Have you found out more about Jenna or Pandora?"

"No. It's Harvey. Well, not Harvey exactly. It's *Carmen*."

"Who's Carmen?"

I explained what had happened earlier.

"Oh." Ruby's eyebrows shot up. "Well, even if they were together once, there's obviously a reason why they split up. I wouldn't worry. Harvey adores you."

"Yes, but they're going to be working with each other for a long time on this recovery," I grumbled. "Very *closely*."

"What's meant to be is meant to be. And you and Harvey *are* definitely meant to be. I can feel it. The Universe is telling me." She gave me a reassuring smile.

"Anyway, what are you doing here so early?" I changed the subject so I could stop thinking about it.

"Ian called me earlier and wanted to know if I'd arrange Pandora's funeral for him, so we're meeting here to discuss it."

"Did you tell him that Pandora was dying of an inoperable brain tumor?"

She nodded gravely. "I did. It was another shock to his system, the poor man. He feels terribly guilty about everything. He realized that's where he knew Dr. Trower's name from, as Ian often sees patients at Seattle Medical Center."

"You know, part of me has been thinking that at least she had a quick and painless death in the end," I said. "From the letter we read, it sounded like the cancer was quite aggressive. She might only have had a few months to live, and the pain she would've gone through would be awful in the end."

"I know what you mean, but it doesn't make it any better that someone took her life."

"No, I agree. I'm not saying that at all. But if the Universe does always have a plan for us, maybe it was the better plan for Pandora."

A knock sounded at the tavern's door, and I went to open it. Ian stood there looking as if he hadn't slept in a long time. There were dark circles underneath his eyes, and his hair stuck up in all directions.

"Hi," I said, wondering again if he was really the killer. "How are you doing?" I stepped back to let him in.

"I've been better."

"Come and sit down." I led him to one of the empty booths. The place wouldn't open for another hour, so we could all talk in private. "We're not doing food yet, but would you like a coffee?"

"That would be lovely, thanks. Espresso. Actually, make it a double, please."

"Gotcha." I turned to Ruby. "Green tea?"

"I'll have a peppermint tea, please."

I headed back to the bar to get the drinks and returned a few minutes later. Ruby had pulled a notepad out of her bag and was asking Ian questions.

"Do you think lilies or roses?"

"Um...I don't know." Ian looked lost, like a helpless child. "Mother used to like roses, but I just didn't know her anymore. That's why I wanted your help."

"Roses then. You can't go wrong with those." Ruby scribbled that down. "I'll make a list of her clients and the few old friends she had to let them know when the funeral is. I'll also make an announcement in the local paper in case any other locals want to pay their respects. Do you want to hold the wake at her house or here?"

"Yes, you're very welcome to have it here," I said, sitting down and sipping my green tea. "I can arrange it all, so you don't need to worry about anything."

"Here, I think." Ian put his chin in his hand and stared out of the window. Today the ocean was choppy, a spray of fine mist floating above it. "I'm going back to Seattle later today. I've got some patients that I need to get back to. I had another look around the house, but I couldn't see anything that might suggest Tim murdered Jenna."

"If Pandora did find something, Tim must've taken it with him before he murdered her," Ruby said.

Ian nodded vacantly. "You're right. I guess that's the end of it now. I just have to accept Jenna really is never coming back." He dug in his pocket and pulled out the keys to Pandora's house, sliding them across the table to Ruby. "I know this is a lot to ask, but could you also organize packing up Mother's things? They can all be sent to the local thrift shop."

"You don't want to keep anything as a reminder?" Ruby asked. "Some of Jenna's things are still there."

"No. I think it's time to finally close the chapter and move on."

"Of course I can, if you're sure." Ruby patted his hand.

"I'm sure." He stared out the window again, and when he spoke, I didn't know if he was talking to us or himself. "At least they've got Tim now. Even if they couldn't prove he killed my sister. At least he's locked up for one murder."

A while later, after Ian and Pandora had finished discussing the funeral arrangements, Vernon arrived. He looked terrible. His skin was pale, but his cheeks were a ruddy complexion, and he walked around the place slowly, wincing every now and then.

"Is your knee playing up?" I asked him, knowing the gunshot wound he'd taken all those years ago still caused him a lot of pain.

"No, I'm good," he said with a forced breath. And with that he sat down at the edge of one of the booths, arms clutched around his stomach, leaning forward.

"You're not okay!" I crouched down in front of him. "What's wrong?"

"I've been getting pains in my stomach. But don't tell Ruby. She'll only cluck around me like a mother hen."

"Don't tell Ruby what?" Ruby appeared, took one look at Vernon's pained face, his clammy forehead, and said, "I knew you'd been hiding something! You need to get to a doctor right now. You look terrible! It's your stomach, isn't it?"

Vernon clenched his teeth and nodded. "I've been having trouble for a while."

"Typical man! Ignore it, and hope it will go away," Ruby muttered, helping him up. "Too much alcohol and an atrocious diet aren't going to help your stomach if it's sensitive. I've been telling you for years, but you never listen to me."

"What did I tell you?" Vernon shot me a look and rolled his eyes at Ruby.

"Well, someone needs to look after you." She linked her arm with his. "I'm taking you to Dr. Eckhardt right this minute." She steered him toward the door before he could object, but judging by the state of him, he looked as if he was way past objecting.

I opened up the tavern in their absence, hoping it was nothing serious. If Vernon did have an ulcer, he'd never hear the end of it from Ruby. And maybe this was the kind of crisis that would finally push them back together again.

In the corner there was a regular crowd of ladies who met once a week here for their bridge club before having lunch. Their glasses were full, so I took the opportunity to look up Melanie Crook in the local directory. Although Jenna hadn't spoken in any detail to Ian about her relationship with Tim, maybe she'd mentioned something to her best friend, Melanie. And perhaps she could shed some light on Ian's own relationship with his sister.

There was no listing for her, but I guessed she'd probably got married in the last twenty years and changed her name. I phoned Ruby instead.

"Hi, is there any news on Vernon?"

"He's in with the doctor now. Silly man." The worry oozed from her voice.

"You know how stubborn he is. This is probably a much-needed wake-up call."

"Most certainly."

"I was just wondering if you knew someone in town called Melanie. She was Jenna's best friend. Used to have the last name Crook, but I can't find her in the book. I wanted to see if she could shed any light on Jenna."

"Oh, yes, Pandora mentioned Melanie once when she was talking about Jenna. She works at a preschool in town, but I'm not sure which one. You could try ringing around them."

"Good idea. Let me know as soon as you hear something about Vernon."

"Will do."

I went through the Yellow Pages, flicking through to the preschools, and found three in Danger Cove. I tried the first one, but they had no one called Melanie working there. I called the second, Happy Tots, and when a woman answered, I asked to speak to Melanie.

"Um...she's teaching in class at the moment. Can I help? Or would you like to leave a message?"

I heard a loud bell ring on the other end of the line.

"Oh, hang on a minute. Break time's just started. Let me see if she's free." She put me on hold, and I listened to some classical music.

A few minutes later another woman came on the line. "Hi, Melanie speaking."

"Oh, hi, my name's Hope Foster, from the Smugglers' Tavern. Did you by any chance used to be Melanie Crook?"

"Yes, that's right. I read in the paper that you and Ruby Fournier found Pandora. It's so sad. Tim Baxtor deserves to rot in hell for what he did."

"Do you have time to speak right now? I'd love to ask you a couple of questions about Jenna and Tim. I'm trying to find out if Pandora discovered something about Jenna that led to her death."

"Well, sure, of course I'll help in any way I can. I always wanted to see him behind bars." A pause. "Hang on for a minute. I'll move to my classroom, where it's more private." There was muffled talking, as if she'd put her hand over the phone. Then I heard the sound of heels clicking on a hard floor and a door opening and closing. "Right. What did you want to know?"

"Ian mentioned that Jenna changed when she was seeing Tim. He said she seemed like she was worried about something before she disappeared. Did she speak to you about anything?"

"Jenna and I went to this very preschool together. We were friends from the first day here, so we were close, you know, more like sisters. But we drifted apart a bit when she got engaged to Tim. He was so controlling, telling her what to wear and that she couldn't go out without him and hang out with her friends. She was madly in love with him, and although I tried to talk to her about the way things were between them, little things I noticed, she didn't listen to me. She couldn't see it. You know what it's like when you're young and in love. You think you know everything, right? But I did see her a couple of days before she disappeared. She said she'd finally woken up and was going to end things with him. She couldn't take it anymore. Said she didn't love him and he was stifling her. She told me she'd been offered a great job in Seattle and he'd told her she couldn't take it, but she was going to anyway. She was looking for a place to live there to get away from him."

"Did she tell you she was meeting him that night at the Fourth of July fair?"

"No. I had the flu then, so I didn't go to the fair. I was at home that night."

"Did Tim ever hit her?"

"Not that I knew of. It was more mental and psychological manipulation, you know? There was one time when we were out in a big group. All Jenna's friends were there. None of Tim's. He never seemed to have any. Anyway, Jenna was chatting with one of the guys who used to be in our class at school, and Tim was furious about it. Called her a whore in front of everyone. She was so embarrassed. They left shortly afterward. He was always hypercritical of things she wore, unreasonably jealous and controlling. And if she wasn't with him, he was constantly phoning her at home to make sure she wasn't hanging out with another guy. It was things like that." She sighed sadly. "The town was divided into two camps: those who thought he'd done it and got away with it and those who thought he was innocent. He put on a good act as the distraught fiancé. I'll give him that." Anger dripped from her words.

"And you thought he'd done something to Jenna?"

"Hell yeah."

"What was Ian's relationship like with Jenna? Did they get on?"

"Ian was six years younger, and they weren't really that close. They didn't argue or anything, but...hey, not all siblings get on, do they? My husband hasn't spoken to his own sister in years. Pandora and Jenna were kind of more like sisters than mother and daughter. They did lots of stuff together."

I thought about Ian telling me they were all a close family at one time. Was that a lie? Or was it wishful thinking? Or distorted memories? "Do you think Ian was jealous of their relationship? That maybe he felt second best?"

She paused for a moment. "I guess, sometimes, maybe. I spent a lot of time at Pandora's with Jenna, and it did seem as if she was her mom's favorite."

Was it possible Ian had become jealous of his sister? Had he felt angry about being left out of the family unit? Did he feel neglected and unloved even then, as if he was competing with Jenna for his mom's attention? And was it enough to make *him* do something to Jenna?

"Can you think of anyone else who might've wanted to harm Jenna? Did someone have a grudge against her? Had she argued with anyone before she disappeared? Was she in some kind of trouble?"

"No, no. Nothing like that. The police asked me all this at the time. Everyone who knew Jenna liked her. I couldn't think of anyone else at the time who would've wanted to do her harm. She wasn't into drinking or drugs or partying. She was always busy with her sketches and designs when she wasn't spending time with Tim. She had everything going for her." She groaned softly. "You know, I loved that girl. I still haven't gotten over her disappearance, so I could understand why Pandora fell apart after what happened. I used to try to visit her afterward, but she didn't want to see anyone."

"So you think Jenna really is dead?"

She didn't hesitate when she said, "Definitely. And I'm really glad they've finally got Tim in custody."

CHAPTER TWELVE

———

An hour later, Ruby and Vernon walked in.

I rushed toward them. "What are you doing here?" I took Vernon's arm. "Shouldn't you be resting or something?"

"That's what I said, but he wouldn't listen," Ruby said.

"It's a suspected ulcer. I'd be bored out of my head sitting at home twiddling my thumbs. The doc's going to schedule some tests for me. It's not like I'm dying or anything."

Ruby's face dropped when he said the *D* word. "It's a wake-up call, is what it is. You need to listen to what your body's telling you. Your gut health is central to your whole body's wellness. An unhealthy digestive system can lead to so many other problems: allergies, chronic fatigue, dementia, cancer, arthritis, eczema, autoimmune diseases. Think of your gut like a rain forest, with its own ecosystem and—"

"A gut ecosystem?" Vernon rolled his eyes at Ruby so hard I'm surprised they didn't plop out. "Seriously?"

Ruby wagged a finger at him. "It's true. You need to look after yourself better."

Vernon put a plastic bag filled with some prescription medicine on the bar top and sat at a stool. He still looked pale and in pain. As if to prove that, he rubbed his stomach and grimaced.

"You need some superfoods. Veggies, healthy protein, vitamins and minerals." She ticked them off on her fingers.

"Yes, thank you, Dr. Fournier," Vernon muttered.

"You are what you eat," Ruby said.

"We're both worried about you," I agreed. "Stop being so stubborn."

"I'm not stubborn!" he said, sounding like a toddler about to throw a tantrum.

"I've told him he should move in with me so I can keep an eye on him. Cook him some healthy things and make sure he eats right."

Vernon grunted. "I'm not a baby."

"Yes, but I know you. You won't take any notice. Right, that's settled, then." Ruby began making arrangements before he could object. "After work we'll go get some of your things and bring them to my place. Starting then, I'm taking care of you. And I'm not taking no for an answer."

I studied Vernon.

He opened his mouth to say something, but then threw his hands into the air, as if it was useless even trying. "Whatever."

* * *

It was early evening when Carmen strutted in looking like a Scandinavian goddess. She'd changed out of her work clothes—if you could call them that—into an ivory silk miniskirt and matching camisole, the light reflecting off the fabric, making it shimmer. She'd catch her death of cold around here dressing like that. She stalked across the floor in ridiculously high heels, heading straight toward me at the bar. She tossed her long blonde mane over her shoulder as she moved, reminding me of a cat. Sleek, smooth, predatory. But then I thought maybe that was insulting to cats.

Down, Hope!

A couple of younger guys nursing bottles of beer perked up when they spotted her, sitting up in their seats and nudging each other. She shot them a sultry smile and sat at the bar, one long tanned leg crossing over the other.

"Hi," I said. "How's the excavation going?"

She shot me a disinterested look. "I don't think I'm at liberty to discuss that with you. Do you have a menu? I'm meeting Harvey for dinner. We've got *so* much to catch up on." The sultry smile turned smug.

I thrust a menu at her before I could smack that smile off her face with it. "Can I get you a drink?"

"Vodka. On the rocks." She glowered at me, fluffing up her hair

"Coming up." I poured her vodka. Thought about pouring it over her head. And when I turned back again, Harvey was there dressed in a pair of faded combats, Converse sneakers, and a long-sleeved black T-shirt. "Hi." I smiled at him, but it wobbled a little on my face. I suddenly felt nervous and less sure of him. Of us.

"Hey." He gave me his signature sexy lopsided grin and said hi to Carmen.

"You'll never guess what I found down there today." Carmen reached out and touched Harvey's hand, letting it linger there a little too long for my liking. "A box of apothecary vessels!"

I didn't have a clue what an apothecary vessel was. Suddenly, I felt stupid and insignificant. I grabbed a bottle of cider from the fridge, poured some ice in a glass, and set it in front of Harvey.

"Oh my God, really?" Harvey's face lit up. "Wow. That's amazing. Are they bottles or porcelain jars?"

"Porcelain. And they're ornately engraved. You *have* to see them!"

He sat down on a stool next to Carmen and twisted to face her. "Wow. I was hoping to find some in amongst all those crates down there. How about British tea? Did you find any of that yet?"

"Not yet. But they don't call me Carmen the Huntress for nothing. If they're there, I'll find them."

I could think of a few other words to call her as my heart sunk into my feet. I wondered whether her "huntress" definition included men. Stupid question, right?

Vernon appeared behind the bar and watched Harvey and Carmen surreptitiously as he polished some glasses.

I served an elderly man a pint of specialty ale and tried not to watch them, too. They looked good together. They obviously had a lot in common with their work. If Carmen was after Harvey, how could I ever compete with her? I turned away, pretending to assess the bar's inventory, and caught my reflection in the mirrored panel above it. I'd never made that much of an effort with my appearance, preferring to use subtle makeup and keep my long waves au naturel, usually with a braid in the front to keep it off my face. I dressed for comfort rather than sexiness or fashion. *Don't get me wrong.* It wasn't like I grew my armpit hair or anything. But I was nothing like the glamorous Carmen, who obviously spent hours in front of a mirror applying her makeup and doing her hair to make it just so. She was polished and immaculately turned out. In contrast, I was kind of frayed around the edges and casual. Maybe it was about time I started paying more attention to my appearance.

With that decided, I turned back to them. "So what can I get you to eat?"

Carmen shot me a dirty look, as if she didn't enjoy the interruption.

"I'm famished." Harvey rubbed his hands together, caught my eye, and winked at me. "What are the specials today, Hope?"

"Um..." The specials had disintegrated from my head suddenly. I felt a bit sick, to be honest, seeing them together.

That smug smile was back on Carmen's face, but it was only for my benefit. It morphed into a friendly one as soon as Harvey turned back to say to her, "The food here is amazing."

Vernon stepped in for me then, rattling the specials off.

"I'll have the prawn coconut curry." Carmen slapped her menu closed. "And then after dinner, how about you show me round the town?" She raised perfectly shaped eyebrows at Harvey, and I made a mental note to pluck mine later. With everything that had happened lately, I'd forgotten.

Harvey glanced at me. "Er...well...I think Hope and I were going to catch up."

"Oh, come on!" Carmen flashed another fake smile at me. "Holly won't mind, will you?"

"It's Hope, actually," I corrected her.

She ignored me and carried on. "I'm new in town, and I'd like to find out where everything is. After all, I'm going to be here a long time with the project." She pouted her red-glossed lips and fluttered her eyelashes at Harvey. I was pretty sure they were way too long to be real.

Harvey swallowed hard, watching me, looking torn.

Of course I mind! But I couldn't let my jealousy show. It would just make Carmen worse. Besides, it was a perfectly normal thing for Harvey to take his colleague around town and get her settled in.

I waved a nonchalant hand. "No, you guys go. We can catch up later." I glanced uneasily at Harvey.

"If you're sure?" Harvey asked. "I can—"

"Of course she is," Carmen butted in.

I tried not to look at them eating their dinner in one of the booths, but my gaze kept straying over there every time Carmen laughed, which she seemed to do a lot. And very loudly.

"You want to watch her," Vernon whispered to me. "She's trouble."

"I know." I wiped down the bar extra vigorously.

It was quiet after Harvey and Carmen left, so Vernon suggested Ruby and I make a start on packing up Pandora's belongings to donate to the thrift shop. Someone would have to collect the furniture, but we could sort out all the smaller personal belongings and anything that needed to be thrown away. I didn't really want to leave Vernon, but he was looking a lot better, and he insisted.

It was dark when we arrived, giving the house an eerie feel. We pulled a pile of flat-pack cardboard boxes and large black trash bags from the trunk of Ruby's car and carried them inside.

Ruby flicked on the lights in the hallway. "We should probably take one room each. Let's start upstairs and work our way down."

"Okay."

Before climbing the stairs, I glanced in the living room, my gaze catching the photos of Jenna on every available surface. Surely Ian would want to keep them. Even though he said he didn't want anything from the house and it might be too painful right now, one day he might want to look at them again.

Ruby decided to start in Pandora's room while I took the smaller one, which was the shrine to Jenna. I opened two boxes.

One for the thrift shop. One for things that we should at least let Ian see before they were destroyed or removed. I had a black trash bag for clothes and another for anything to throw away.

I folded up her clothes neatly and placed them in one bag, along with her shoes, bags, and belts. In the drawers, I found underwear, socks, and swimsuits, which went in the trash.

I removed Jenna's sketches from the walls and carefully placed them in Ian's box, then sat at the small stool in front of the dressing table. I opened her jewelry box, pulling out the tangle of items, the crystal bracelets, the silver charm bracelet, earrings. Would Ian want these too? I doubted it. It all looked like costume or inexpensive jewelry to me. I put it all back in the jewelry box and added that to the thrift pile.

I was just removing the sheets and pillowcases from the bed to throw into the trash bag hours later, when Ruby appeared.

"I've finished Pandora's room." She sat down on the bed. "I've still got the spare room to do, which used to be Ian's."

"This one's done too." I sat next to her. "We can come back another time and finish it off."

"So sad." She glanced around, then patted my leg. "Come on. Let's take these boxes and load them into the car."

Ten minutes later we'd lugged the boxes and bags downstairs and were driving into town to drop them off at the rear entrance to the thrift store, which was not open at this time of night. As we drove past the Irish bar, Flannagan's, on Main Street, I spotted Carmen exiting, closely followed by Harvey. She looked pretty drunk, wobbly on her high heels. She grabbed hold of Harvey's arm and laughed.

I let out a deep growl.

CHAPTER THIRTEEN

———

The following morning I phoned The Clip and Sip hair salon. With everything that had been happening in the last few months, I'd neglected myself for too long. *Way* too long, thinking about it. I hadn't set foot in a salon for years. Bob's daughter, Elise, had called me a hippie freak, although I preferred the term boho chic. I wasn't used to spending much time on my appearance. When I was traveling the world, it wasn't like I could haul a hairdryer and endless supplies of lotions and potions around, so I'd perfected the minimalist wash-and-go look. At least I thought I had. But now with Carmen in the picture, I figured it was definitely time for a little makeover.

The salon was newly refurbished and welcoming, which was a relief. I always felt nervous coming into places like this, as if people were judging me.

A curvy blonde was behind the desk, on the phone. She flashed me a sunny smile, revealing perfectly white teeth, and carried on talking, noting down an appointment. Another member of the staff, who had heavily applied makeup and wore a cheetah-print dress with a name tag that read *Gia* on it, was styling the only other customer in the place.

The woman on the phone hung up and turned to me. "Hi, I'm Cassidi, the new owner. How can I help?"

"I'm Hope." I returned the smile. "I booked an appointment earlier."

"Great! Follow me." She led me to a comfy chair in front of a mirror along the side wall, next to the window.

I sat down and watched her in the mirror as she picked up chunks of my waves. "When did you last have it cut?"

"Um...about two years ago." I laughed.

"Wow! Well, it's in great condition. Just a few split ends that need attention. Did you want just a trim or a restyle?" She carried on running her fingers through it, pulling the ends around my shoulders as she examined it. "I think the length really suits you. Maybe you could have a few layers put in? It would frame your face and make it pop. What do ya think?"

"Sounds perfect."

"Do you want me to weave in some highlights or lowlights?"

"I'm not sure."

"I can make them subtle, just to enhance your own color?" She opened a color chart book and pointed to two samples. "I'm thinking something like chocolate brown and caramel. What do you think?"

"What the hell? Why not!"

"Okay, then. I'll mix up 'em up and be right back."

A few minutes later, she wheeled a small trolley toward me, laden with bowls of dye and sections of foil. "Can I get you anything to drink before we start?" She handed me a menu. "I do a mean limoncello." She flashed those perfect teeth at me again. "Make it myself from scratch."

I took the menu from her and studied it. "A limoncello would be great, thanks."

She disappeared, and I looked out the window while I waited. The stop sign at the end of the street caught my eye. It was leaning at a forty-five-degree angle onto the sidewalk.

"Here you go." Cassidi set a cocktail glass in front of me.

I took a sip of deliciousness: sweet, tart, zesty, all rolled into one. "This is amazing. I bet my customers would love this. Do you have any more I can buy for the tavern?" I took another sip, rolling the flavor over my tongue, already thinking about the kind of cocktail I could make with it.

"I've got bottles of the stuff."

We agreed on a price for the limoncello while she worked her magic on my hair, taking sections of it and applying dye before wrapping them in foil packets. Then she said, "Did you see that stop sign? Some maniac ran into it the other day and just drove off." She shot me a *can you believe it* look and combed through another section of hair. "I heard the skid and then *bang!* Straight into it!"

"Well, at least it did its job." I laughed.

"He was driving too fast." She wagged the end of her applicator brush at me. "He could've knocked someone over. Some guy in a flashy red Range Rover."

A tingling feeling traveled over my scalp that had nothing to do with Cassidi's fingers. How many red Range Rovers had I seen in Danger Cove in the year I'd been here? One. And that belonged to Ian Williams. "Did you see the guy driving it?"

"Oh yeah. He got out of his car to check the front of it. He was kind of skinny, with lots of freckles and strawberry-blond hair that needed a cut."

It sounded like Ian.

"I even got the plate number in case the police wanted to know. That stop sign's dangerous now, right? It could fall on someone."

"When was this, exactly?"

She told me, and I calculated backward. Yep, it was the day before Pandora had been killed.

"Can you give me the plate number before I go? I think it was the same guy who nearly ran me off the road on my bike." Oops, another little lie slipped out. I was going to have to do some seriously good deeds to get my good karma store back up.

She shrugged. "Sure. It was a vanity plate. *Cardio1.*"

* * *

As I was passing back through town, I spotted Bernie Templeton's occult shop. I'd bought some candles and crystals from her before, and since I never did end up getting my crystal healing session with Pandora, I had a sudden urge to stop there. I was usually a well-grounded person, confident in myself, and had nurtured self-love over the years I'd been traveling the world. When I left the commune at eighteen, I'd seen myself as worthless and unlovable, and it had taken years of doing work on myself to change the way my childhood had shaped me. Change the way I thought about myself. But sometimes it's not easy to maintain positivity and keep away the doubts and anxiety. I needed more of...well, something. Something to remind me I was a worthy person. Something to stop me being jealous of Carmen. I needed a boost of confidence.

I opened the door to the small, darkened shop and was greeted with a powerful smell of incense and herbs. It instantly reminded me of being back in India and the Far East, wandering around the bustling, colorful street markets, meditating at the yoga retreat where I'd first met Ruby. A bell chimed above me as I shut the door again and looked around. I browsed the candles in all shapes, colors, and sizes. There were wicker baskets full of dried flowers and herbs that I picked up and sniffed, letting them work their sensory magic.

Bernie appeared from behind a dark-blue velvet curtain at the back of the shop. She was tall and slim, her brown hair swishing against her chin as she walked behind the counter. "Hi, Hope. Haven't seen you for a while." She smiled warmly.

"I know. Way too long."

"Did you want some more candles? I just got some new stock in."

My gaze drifted toward the display of crystals on top of the counter. More wicker baskets housed all kinds of different shapes and colors. On a hanging rack next to them were crystal bracelets, necklaces, and earrings. "Actually, I wanted to get something to enhance confidence and balance."

Bernie's smile didn't waver, although her eyes assessed me calmly and confidently, as if she was trying to read some kind of vibrational energy around me. She nodded with understanding. "What are you drawn to?" She tilted her head toward the crystals.

I picked up a tiger's-eye bracelet, the bands of golds, browns, and oranges running through it. "This is beautiful."

"Good choice. It's powerful for aiding harmony and inner balance. Also helps you release any fear and anxiety." She picked up a lump of tiger's-eye from the basket, smoothing her finger over it. "Traditionally, people carried it as an amulet to protect against curses and ill-wishing by others."

I thought about Carmen. Yes, I definitely needed a hefty dose of protection from her.

"It also gives you courage and enhances self-confidence. And its energy is very powerful, helping you work through difficult times and challenges. A perfect crystal for grounding you."

"Sold!" I grinned, handing her the bracelet. "This is exactly what I need. You don't need to wrap it, thanks. I'll wear it."

"Okay. Are you looking for anything else? Or perhaps you'd like a tarot reading?"

"Sure, why not, while I'm here?"

"Excellent. Follow me out back."

I stepped behind the curtain into a small, private room. A stained glass lamp gave off a subtle, relaxing ambience, filtering colors against the floor and walls with an ethereal glow. Wooden bookcases were crammed in every available space, shelves filled full of occult books, crystal bibles, and numerous different packs of cards: Angel Cards, Oracle Cards, Animal Cards, Goddess Guidance Cards, Butterfly Cards.

"Please sit and make yourself comfortable."

I sat in a rattan chair draped with a colorful throw. An incense stick burned in a holder on the matching table in front of me, the smoke wafting about a lovely smell of vanilla.

"There are many spreads I can do that cover things like relationships, plotting goals, or answering specific questions you have. Or, one of the most popular, is the six-card spread, which is a great reading to get a snapshot of how things are going in your life generally at this moment."

The relationship spread was tempting, but what if it told me something about Harvey and me that I didn't want to know? The question spread sounded good, but my specific question would be who killed Pandora and Jenna, and I doubted I would get a clear answer. I settled for the six-card spread instead.

Bernie handed me a pack of colorful, well-used cards and told me to shuffle them. "You can also ask a specific question with this spread, or just let your mind go blank and let the cards do the work, offering up what you need to know at this present moment."

I shuffled away, trying to empty my mind and just let the cards give me their guiding message.

"When you're ready, just pick six cards and lay them face down on the table."

I did as I was told.

"Okay." She smiled. "Let's see what we have." She turned over the first card. "This card signifies how you feel about yourself."

Great. It was *The Fool*.

"Relax." She noticed the frown edging across my forehead. "This one means that you feel uneasy or discontent at the moment. Maybe you need a change, a new adventure, or new direction. It usually means you're unsure how things stand. You may not know where you want to go or what you want to do. But it's also a time of optimism and making decisions. You need to ask yourself if what you want is really the right thing for you. Unexpected influences could have a powerful effect on whatever you decide."

What did that mean? Was Carmen the unexpected influence? Was Harvey really right for me? Oh God. Maybe I shouldn't have started this.

Bernie turned over the next card. *The Hanged Man*. Uh-oh, this was getting worse and worse.

"This signifies what you want most right now."

"Well, I definitely haven't been thinking of hanging myself." I worriedly eyed the picture of a man hanging from a tree.

She laughed. "Of course not. This card suggests that perhaps you think things aren't going as planned at the moment. But you don't want to give someone or something up. You need to trust that this moment is just the passage of one stage in your life to another. Whatever the outcome, things will resolve themselves to your benefit in the end."

Hmmm, so that was good, right?

The next card she turned over was *Strength*. "This represents your fears. You're scared of lacking the strength and courage to deal with someone who's bothering you."

Carmen again?

"If you listen to your fears, it will only create failure, and opportunities could be lost. You need to find your inner strength.

The courage of a lion within you. Be brave." She turned over the next card.

Death.

"I'm not really liking the whole *Hanged Man* and *Death* thing. There's a bit of a pattern emerging." I tried to make my voice sound jokey.

"This is what you've got going for you at the moment."

"What, death?" Maybe it was a message in relation to Pandora's murder or Jenna's disappearance instead and nothing to do with me at all. I hoped.

"It represents endings and new beginnings. Your life is going through a time of transformation. And while it may be a rocky road, eventually you'll pull through to start a brand-new chapter in your life."

But did that chapter include Harvey? Or...uh-oh...was the rocky road about Lester arresting me again for getting involved in his investigation?

The next card was *The Magician.*

"This is what's going against you." She tapped the card. "Someone isn't quite what they seem. Their deception is cleverly disguised beneath charm and friendliness."

Hmmm...that definitely summed up Carmen.

"Be cautious and trust your instincts."

She flipped the final card. *The High Priestess.*

"This represents the likely outcome for you. Your intuition is coming into play now. You need to carefully listen to and trust it. If you do this, you'll make the right decisions. You need to be flexible, but you can expect a promising outcome."

* * *

I hurried back to the tavern on my bike, not really any the wiser. The tarot cards seemed a bit conflicting to me. My intuition told me Carmen was bad news. But how could I compete with her?

I hoped the ride wouldn't make the new bouncy, vibrant locks Cassidi had given me look like I'd been left in a wind tunnel. Running my hand through it after I stashed my bike, I headed inside and grabbed Ruby and Vernon, pulling them into my office.

"You'll never guess what," I said.

"You've had your hair done?" Vernon said. "Looks great, by the way."

"It looks amazing!" Ruby agreed.

I caught my reflection in the mirror. My hair now cascaded past my shoulders in glossy, layered waves with subtle hints of color reflecting the light. And now that I was armed with my tiger's-eye bracelet, there was no way Carmen would turn Harvey against me. Right?

I turned back to them. "No, it's not the hair, but thanks anyway. It's about Ian. Didn't he say he hadn't been in Danger Cove for years?"

"Yes," Ruby said. "Why?"

"Well, it seems that his car was involved in a minor traffic accident outside the Clip and Sip the day before Pandora was killed. That's only two streets away from Pandora's house."

A twinkle sparkled in Vernon's eye. "Interesting."

"It is strange," Ruby said thoughtfully. "But that doesn't mean he actually saw Pandora. Maybe he came into town for another reason. To see a patient or something."

"But why did he lie about it?" Which got me thinking about the open rear door in Pandora's kitchen again. What if Tim was telling the truth and Pandora was really alive when he left? In the five minutes we waited to go inside her house, Ian could've slipped in the back door, killed her, and slipped out again. And, as a doctor, he had easy access to the pentobarbital. "Ian is Pandora's sole heir, after all."

"I don't know," Ruby said. "Ian seemed like a lovely guy who's been through a lot."

"Yeah, but money does strange things to people," Vernon said.

"He could've been in town seeing a friend," Ruby suggested.

"Then why lie about it?" Vernon repeated.

"And I got hold of Melanie Crook too. She was Jenna's best friend at the time she went missing, and she told me that she thought Jenna was Pandora's favorite and Ian always felt left out, even before Jenna disappeared. Maybe Ian killed Jenna because he was jealous of her. Then maybe he killed Pandora to get her inheritance, and framed Tim."

"Or to shut Pandora up because she'd found out the truth about Ian killing Jenna," Vernon added.

"But Ian wanted us to pack up everything from Pandora's house to give to the thrift shop. If he was out to kill his mom for money, he showed no interest in her belongings," Ruby said.

"Judging by the old and outdated items in the house, we didn't see anything valuable in there," I said. "And he did mention he'd gone back there again on his own, so maybe he took whatever items were worth something then."

"We need to find out if Ian's got an alibi for the time of Pandora's murder," Vernon said.

"How can we do that without directly asking him?" I asked. "We don't want to let him know we think he could be a suspect."

Vernon rubbed his jaw, pondering that for a moment. "We can start by calling his office to see if he was working that day, then take it from there."

"I'll do it."

"Lester Marshall gave me Ian's work, home, and cell numbers," Ruby said. "I wrote them down on the pad." She pointed to the notepad on my desk.

Ruby and Vernon went out front to serve while I punched in the number. A recorded message played in my ear. "Thank you for calling the Seattle Cardio Clinic. Our offices are closed for our annual Labor Day holiday between Monday, September 7th, and Thursday, September 10th. If you have an emergency, please call the Beckwith Health Surgery on this number—"

I hung up before she could finish. Of course! The Labor Day holiday had been on Monday, which was why we'd been so busy. Since the tavern was always open on holidays, the days kind of rolled into one for me. The owners of the clinic had obviously decided to give the staff a few extra days off afterward, which meant he hadn't been working on the day he hit the stop sign, the day after the official public holiday. And he hadn't been working the next day, either, when she was murdered, according to the dates on the message. But that didn't mean he didn't have an alibi.

I pulled Vernon aside to let him know. He disappeared into my office to do some more digging and see what else he could find out.

Bree Milford, manager of the Ocean View Bed and Breakfast, where Harvey and Carmen were staying, wandered in then with her best friend, Cristal.

"Hi, Hope," Bree said while Cristal popped her hand up in a cheerleader sort of acknowledgement. "Can I take a menu, and we'll sit outside for an early dinner?"

"Sure." I handed one to each of them and told them the specials. "How's business?"

"It's been crazy busy, what with Labor Day and all. I hardly get out these days since I took over the B&B. It's a big change from LA, but still, it's good. I enjoy it."

"Well, life's too short. You gotta enjoy what you do and have fun," I said.

"Cheers to that," Cristal said.

I took their drink orders, and they sat outside while I made them both the specialty cocktail of the house, a Smugglers' Pink Parrot. When I got outside to their table, Bree was watching Carmen emerging from the privacy tent.

"How's Harvey getting on with his work?" Bree asked me, not taking her eyes off Carmen. It felt like a loaded question, as if she wanted to tell me something.

"Yeah, good. Busy, though. Aren't we all?" I laughed.

Cristal spun toward me. "I know I shouldn't talk about the guests, but I'll be glad when she's gone." She nodded toward Carmen. "She woke several of the other guests up at about three this morning, banging on Harvey's door."

"Three a.m.?" I asked. What was she doing trying to get hold of Harvey at that time in the morning?

"I mentioned something to her at breakfast, and she didn't like it," Cristal said. "She was so rude and condescending, speaking to me like I was an idiot. But we can't let her disturb everyone else, right?"

"That's right," Bree said. "Cristal told me about it this morning. I didn't hear a thing from my apartment over the garage."

A nauseous feeling swirled inside as I looked back and forth between them. "So what um...happened? I mean...did Harvey let her in at that time?"

Cristal's mouth turned down at the edges with sympathy. "I don't know. She was banging for about five minutes, and it woke me up too. I was just about to get up and investigate, when I heard some hushed voices, and it stopped, so I don't know what happened afterward."

I forced a smile, while my insides were in turmoil, as I pulled my order pad from my apron. Were those tarot cards literal meanings? Was I *The Fool*, thinking Harvey and I were meant to be together, when we really weren't suited? Was he still in love with Carmen? I shook the thoughts away, summoning up my inner lion like Bernie had mentioned. *Do not let your old anxieties bloom. You are worthy. And Harvey is not interested in Carmen. They're just colleagues. I am the lion! Be the lion!* I did an inner roar, picturing a lion's face, and said, "So what can I get you?"

Hours later though, I was still wondering what could've been so urgent that Carmen wanted to talk to Harvey in his bedroom at ridiculous-o-clock in the morning. I very much doubted it was to do with work, unless she wanted to check his tool kit was in good working order!

And did Harvey let her in?

No, of course he didn't. Harvey's not like that. He wouldn't cheat on you. He's a nice guy.

Yeah, but how well do you really know him? You thought you knew Nick, and he cheated.

I was twirling a lock of hair around my finger, lost in thought, when Vernon tapped me on the shoulder.

I jumped.

"Sorry, didn't mean to scare you," he said.

"You've been miles away all evening," Ruby said. "What's up?"

I waved my hand. "Oh, nothing. Just...no, it doesn't matter. What's meant to be is meant to be, right?"

Ruby looked at me quizzically, but before she could say anything else, Vernon spoke.

"I've found out something interesting. It turns out Ian was given a speeding ticket by Officer Faria on the road leading out to Seattle at 4:10 p.m. on the day Pandora was killed."

"Wow! First the stop sign, then a speeding ticket. He's a really bad driver," Ruby said. "Remind me never to get on a road when he's around."

"But that can't be a coincidence, can it? Ten minutes after we found Pandora dead, he was being stopped not far from her house." For once I was glad about Richie Faria's overzealous pursuit of traffic violations.

"No way." Vernon shook his head. "We need to take a closer look at Ian's finances. Maybe he was after Pandora's money, and her will gives him a motive. There was a five-minute window of opportunity before you went inside the house, when he could've killed her. And what better way to do it than frame Tim Baxtor, who's the perfect suspect?"

"Yes, but that would mean Ian had to have known Tim was going to the house at that exact time," Ruby said.

"Not if Ian was the one who really made that phone call to Tim," I said. "Tim hadn't spoken to Pandora for years, so maybe he couldn't remember exactly what she sounded like. He could've distorted his voice somehow."

"It's not impossible," Vernon said. "You can buy software that changes your voice. Ian could've made that call, then sat ready and waiting for Tim to leave and then kill Pandora for the inheritance."

Ruby tapped her fingernails on the bar, thinking. "I don't know. I still think Tim's the most likely suspect, but I admit that the theft of the pentobarbital from the vet is an unlikely coincidence."

"Does Lester Marshall know about Ian being in the area?" I asked Vernon.

"I doubt it. He's convinced Tim's the killer. Knowing Marshall, he won't be doing any extra work to check out other possibilities."

"I should go and tell him."

"Yeah. Good luck with that." Vernon grunted. "Anyway, I'll carry on looking into Ian's background. See what I can find."

"Can you look after things here?" I asked Ruby.

"Of course."

I grabbed my bag and walked around the side of the building to get my bike. Carmen wasn't anywhere in sight near the entrance to the caves, although her equipment was laid out on the ground next to it. With any luck she'd fallen in and broken her leg.

Uh-oh. Now I was having seriously nasty thoughts. What was wrong with me? I believed that we were what we thought. What we put out there, we got back. The good and the bad. I sent a silent message to the Universe to retrieve it before it sent a humongous karma bus to slam into me in return.

I was just grabbing my bike, when I noticed an envelope on the doorstep at the outer door to my apartment. It was white, weighted down by a rock to stop it flying away in the breeze. I smiled as I removed the rock and picked it up. Maybe it was a note from Harvey, although looking at the writing, which said *HOPE* in big blocky capitals, I didn't think so.

I ripped it open, read it, and a little gasp slipped out. There were only two sentences, but they packed a mean punch:

STAY AWAY. I'M WATCHING YOU!

My throat dried up as I glanced around, wondering if whoever wrote it was actually watching me now, but there was no one in the vicinity. I cycled down Craggy Hill to the police station, heart thumping, although that had less to do with the exercise and more to do with the threatening note. I skidded to a stop outside and leaned my bike against the front steps, rushing inside. Officer Richie Faria was manning the front desk, his uniform so starched it looked as if it could probably stand up on its own.

"I need to see Lester Marshall urgently," I burst out.

"Let me see if *Detective* Marshall is available. He's very busy at the moment." He disappeared down the corridor and rushed back a few minutes later. "Follow me." He led me to the detectives' office. Lester was sitting at the only occupied desk, feet up on it as he fiddled with his cell phone and shoved pizza into his mouth.

Busy, huh?

"Well, I've got speeding tickets to write up, but if you need me for anything, I can hang around." Richie looked eagerly at Lester.

Lester chewed vigorously and waved his hand in a *leave it to me* gesture.

Richie's face fell, and he stomped back to the front desk.

I sat down in front of Lester, waiting for him to finish chewing. He put his cell phone on top of his briefcase on the desk, took a swig of coffee from a full mug, then sat back in his chair, hands on the arms. "To what do I owe the pleasure?" Although his tone was pretty clear that it wasn't a pleasure. The feeling was mutual.

"I just received this threatening note. It was left on my doorstep." I handed him the envelope.

He eyed me suspiciously. "Place it on the desk."

I did as he asked while he opened his drawer and grabbed some latex gloves. He pulled them on with a slapping sound, then opened the envelope, reading.

He glanced up at me. "Anyone else touched this apart from you?"

"No. I came straight here."

He pulled out a plastic evidence bag from his drawer and plopped the note and envelope inside. "And do you have any reason why someone would threaten you?"

"Because of Pandora's death," I said.

He scrunched his face up in a scowl, nostrils flaring. Yep, definitely a gorilla face. "I knew it! You're butting in on my investigation, aren't you?" He leaned forward, threading his fingers together. "What did I tell you?"

"Look, someone's threatened me! So it must mean that you're wrong and Tim isn't the murderer, mustn't it? This was hand delivered, and Tim couldn't have done that from jail. Which means someone else killed Pandora, and Tim was set up like he claims." I blew out a frustrated breath. "Someone's trying to stop me digging any further."

"Yes. Me. Because it's a *police* investigation!" His face turned a dangerous shade of...well, I wasn't sure what it was, really. Neon watermelon, maybe? "We can't have gung-ho citizens stirring people up and poking their noses into investigations! And if you're not careful, you'll end up in the cell next to Tim Baxtor!" He vigorously wagged a finger at me.

"Are you okay?" I eyed him carefully. He looked as if he could easily burst a blood vessel any second.

"No, I'm not okay. I'm investigating a murder, and I've got Miss Marple on my tail!" His face turned redder.

"I think you should get your blood pressure checked. Or maybe do some meditating. It's great for relieving stress and—"

"Shut up, and let me speak!"

"I'm only trying to help."

"What part of shut up don't you understand? Now zip it while I talk!"

I sat back and rested my hands in my lap, suitably chastised.

He let out an angry sigh, which probably could've been heard all the way to Seattle, and said, "Tim could've easily got a friend to write this. It doesn't prove anything."

I thought about his wife, Donna. Had she sent the note? "Okay, maybe." But no, that didn't seem to fit. "But if Tim was innocent, then he'd *want* people to be asking questions, wouldn't he? He'd want the real killer to be caught, so he wouldn't be threatening me to back off." *There, take that, Lester. That blows your theory out the window, hey?* I carried on talking while I could get a word in. "And did you know that Pandora's son, Ian, was in town the day before Pandora's death, even though he told us he hadn't been back to Danger Cove for years? He had a minor traffic accident when he ran into a stop sign outside the Clip and Sip. And also—"

"Is the sign damaged?" Lester sat up straighter, suddenly appearing interested.

"What?"

"The stop sign. Is there any damage? I'm sure Officer Faria would love to follow it up if it is. Damage to town property is an offense."

I waved an exasperated hand around. Is that all he was worried about? "That's not important at the moment. What—"

"I'll decide what's important or not, Ms. Foster. Now, is it damaged?"

"Well, a little bit, but he was also in town on the *actual* day Pandora was murdered. Officer Faria gave him a speeding ticket at ten past four on the road that leads out of Danger Cove. That was ten minutes after we found her body. So what I'm trying to say is that Ian lied to me about not being in town. Why would he do that if he wasn't involved in Pandora's death? You have to admit the timing is weird. If he hadn't seen his mom for years, then suddenly visits the day before and on the day of her death, what happened? What is he trying to hide?"

"That he ran into a stop sign and didn't report it?" Lester said. "And that he needs to go on a speed-awareness course?" Lester scribbled something down in a notepad on his desk. "I'll get Officer Faria onto·that right away."

"Don't you think it's suspicious?" I couldn't help thinking that Ian's sudden arrival had somehow sparked off Pandora's death. What if they'd argued about something? Then maybe he'd hatched a plan to come back and kill her and frame Tim Baxtor. There was something about Tim's involvement that just seemed too...perfect. Too choreographed. Ian could've used a throwaway phone to lure Tim to Pandora's house, then slipped inside the back door after Tim left but before we arrived.

"I think it's an offense, and we'll be having words with him about it if there's any damage to the stop sign."

"So you'll speak to him? Find out what he was doing here? Why he was seen a couple of streets away from Pandora's the day before she was murdered? Ask him why minutes later he was speeding away from the very town where his mom was murdered?"

Lester began shuffling some papers on his untidy desk with a bored expression on his face. "We have the murderer in custody, and he's going to be arraigned later today. The evidence is very clear. If I were you, I'd get back to *bartending* and leave the real police work to the professionals."

I was really good then. I didn't even snort. It took a lot of effort though.

"And what about the threatening note? Will you check to see if there are any prints on it?"

"Yeah, yeah." He waved me away. "But don't expect too much. We're busy trying to put a case together against Baxtor. That'll take priority." He bent his head over the desk and picked up his phone, pressing buttons like he was sending a text. He glanced up when I hadn't moved. "Are you still here?"

"Don't you need to take *my* prints to compare with any you find on the note?"

"We already have them on file, from when you were arrested before."

I thought back to my initial arrest for Bob's murder, before I was vindicated. "Oh yeah."

"And you'd better get out of here now before I arrest you again for obstruction of justice or interfering with witnesses or"—he shrugged casually—"something."

I turned on my heels and walked out of his office, then stuck my tongue out at him through the wall. Childish, maybe, and even though he couldn't see me, it made me feel better. The guy was so frustrating! And an idiot. And lots of other things that were probably too rude to name. What I really wanted to do was whack some sense into him, batter him over the head with his briefcase, but knowing Lester, there would be nothing in it apart from junk food, and that wouldn't be heavy enough for what I had in mind. Instead, I breathed deeply, muttering a calming mantra to hopefully channel some more positive, relaxed energy.

CHAPTER FOURTEEN

———

I was so deep in thought as I dropped off my bike and walked around the outside of the tavern toward the pub garden that I didn't see Carmen until she called out to me.

"Oy, Holly or...whatever your name is!" she yelled.

I stopped. Turned around, suppressing a growl that she'd got my name wrong yet again. She was totally doing it on purpose. Her shorts were even tinier today, if that was possible. Her cleavage was just about held in by her skimpy tank top, but I wouldn't want to take bets on those puppies actually staying in there when she started working. She couldn't have been more obvious if she'd been screaming "Come and get me!" at the top of her voice.

"Oh, hey." I forced a smile. *Be calm. Be patient. Send her peace and love thoughts.* "How's the dig going?"

"Very well," she said, doing that *eyeing me up and down* thing again. She peered closer at me with a glacial grin on her face. "I'd sue your hairdresser if I were you. That cut looks really uneven. And...those highlights are green!"

A hand instinctively went to my new haircut and smoothed down the waves. It wasn't uneven at all. And it definitely didn't look green. Bitch.

Okay, sorry, Universe. I know that was really nasty, but, can you blame me?

I wanted to wipe that grin off her face. I'd learned Muay Thai boxing in Thailand and kung fu in China, and I did a mean uppercut and spinning backfist that could easily render someone unconscious, especially if she weren't expecting a five-foot-three-inch bartender to be on the other end of the blow. I was torn between wanting to do one of those moves or simply punching her. They were all pretty tempting. I couldn't let her walk all over me. But that would make me just as bad as her.

Rise above it, Hope! Do not give her the satisfaction of letting her know she's got to you.

"Is that what you wanted to tell me?" I folded my arms across my chest to stop from slapping her. Keeping my inner anger from popping out was hard going when she was around. I summoned up a supreme smile.

Peace and love. Peace and love.

"Actually, I have a message from Harvey. He's found a section of the hull from the *Ocean's Revenge*, so it looks like he's going to be tied up with recovering that for the rest of the day. He told me to tell you he'd have to cancel your dinner plans. What a shame!" She gave me one of her signature smug smiles that bared a little too much teeth for my liking. She reminded me of a snapping crocodile, lying in wait with that creepy grin on its face, vicious teeth poking out either side, just waiting for the right moment when its prey was close by to strike. "You don't mind, do you?" A sneer crinkled up her face as she crossed her arms around her cleavage.

I did mind. Lately, Harvey and I never seemed to have a minute alone. And with Carmen butting into our lives, and maybe Harvey's bedroom, I minded a hell of a lot. But I'd never give her the satisfaction of letting it show. Anyway, this was Harvey's job. An important find that could blow his career sky high. I wasn't about to ruin things for him. Still, it didn't help my wish that Carmen would suddenly be called back to England and get out of our lives, because if Harvey had now found what he'd been searching for, it meant Carmen would probably be sticking around too. Great! "No, of course I don't mind. This is important for Harvey," I said as casually as I could, trying hard to hide the crack in my voice. I didn't want to sound desperate.

"Exactly. Far more important than any date with you." She tossed her long hair over her shoulders, a haughty gleam in her eyes.

I ignored her snarky barb and left her there, her words ringing in my ears as I headed inside the tavern. Ruby was at the bar, serving a coffee to Elizabeth Ashby, the famous Danger

Cove author who came in sometimes with her notebook and pen and whiled away a few hours, writing with deep concentration. I always wondered if she was using the locals as character material for her books.

"Hi, Elizabeth, how are you?" I asked, stepping behind the bar, forcing my anger at Carmen back down.

She gave me a huge smile. "Everything's great. How are you?" She glanced around. "I'm so glad Bob left this place to you. It looks like business is going well."

"Very well, thanks. Are you working on a new book?"

She tapped her nose secretively. "Always." She took her coffee to one of the booths, pulled out her notebook from a quilted bag, and began scribbling with earnest.

"How did you get on with Lester?" Ruby turned to me, hand on hip.

"As you'd expect, really. The only thing he's concerned about is whether Ian damaged the stop sign! He's not interested in checking whether he's got an alibi or not. And before I got there, I received a threatening note!"

"What?" Her mouth fell open. "What did it say?"

I told her. "So I think that proves my theory that someone other than Tim killed Pandora, and we must be on the right track. Someone's getting rattled."

Ruby bit her lip, eyes misting with worry. "Look, maybe we should just stop this and let Lester handle it. I don't want anything to happen to you."

"We can't. At least I can't. I'd hate to think of someone being wrongly convicted and sent to prison for the rest of his life. Or worse, getting the death penalty. And you know as well as me that Lester's not looking any further than Tim. Anyway, I can look after myself." I wasn't overly worried about being able to protect myself with my martial arts training. Okay, maybe just a little. A vision of me doing one of those moves on Carmen sprang into my head again, but I trampled the thought down. I didn't want to think about her. It would just give credence to her bitchiness.

"Is Lester running prints on the threatening note?"

"Probably not in this century. So again, it's up to us to find out the truth."

"Well, you be careful, and stay alert."

"I will."

"Vernon's been in your office on the laptop since you left, looking into Ian's background."

"Great. Let's hope he comes up with something that might help." I grabbed a bottle of water from the fridge and glugged thirstily. "Maybe we should also take a closer look at Donna. What if she knew Tim was going to see Pandora that day and didn't like it? They work together in the pharmacy, don't they? Tim could've told her Pandora had contacted him, and Donna didn't want all the accusations being resurrected again, which would ruin their business and reputation. She could've had a motive to shut Pandora up."

"By framing her husband?"

I shrugged. "Maybe she's not as angry and upset about his arrest as it seemed when I saw her talking to Bud Ohlsen. It could all be an act. I think I need to go to the pharmacy and see her. See what I can find out." I turned to a couple of guys who'd approached the bar and served them a pitcher of beer. Then I said to Ruby, "Carmen just told me Harvey's found some of the wreckage from the *Ocean's Revenge*."

"Really? Wow! That's great for him."

"Yes." I tried to sound enthusiastic. It was huge for him.

"But?" She tilted her head in a question.

"But it means Carmen will be here longer, and it's obvious she wants him back."

Ruby put an arm around my shoulder and hugged me toward her. "It takes two to tango, as they say. And I'm certain Carmen isn't on Harvey's dance card anymore. Harvey's besotted with you."

"I don't know," I mumbled, fiddling with my tiger's-eye bracelet.

She hugged me tighter. "Stop worrying about something that might not happen."

"It's just that he's the first guy I've liked for a long time. The only one I've taken a chance on since Nick. I don't want to get hurt again. Maybe I should just stop things with him now before I get any deeper involved."

"Sometimes you have to take a leap of faith and put yourself out there."

"What, like you and Vernon? It's obvious you two still love each other, and look at you guys."

Ruby stiffened and stared out of the window with a sad expression, as if remembering their past relationship. Ruby had been a witness in a case Vernon was working on when they'd met, and he'd saved her life. In the process, Vernon had been shot in the knee in the line of duty, and his fast-tracked career in the FBI took a nosedive when he was moved to desk duties. After they became involved romantically, Vernon's pride came between them, and he'd thought Ruby was only with him because she felt pity for him. Sadly, things hadn't worked out between them, but it was never too late to try again.

"Love doesn't always conquer all, you know," Ruby muttered, shaking her head.

"Exactly. Especially when you've got someone like Carmen breathing down your neck."

"Why don't you have a heart to heart with Harvey and tell him how you feel?" She swung around to face me.

"Because I don't think Harvey can see what she's like. When he's around, she's smiley and friendly, but when he's not there, her true colors come out. And I don't want to come across like a jealous girlfriend."

She gave me a sympathetic smile. "What's that saying? If you love someone, set them free. If they come back, they're yours. If not, they never were? You can't *make* someone love you, or manipulate them into being with you if they don't want to."

"I know that. And I wouldn't want to, either."

"I'm not talking about you. I'm talking about Carmen."

"Well, maybe that works just as well with you and Vernon. His health scare has thrown you together in the same house now. It could be a sign that you should both try again."

Just then Vernon rushed from the corridor that led to my office, with a grin plastered on his face. "It turns out that Ian isn't just a cardiologist at the Seattle clinic. He actually owns it. But the business hasn't been doing well lately. I went through his finances, and it seems he's been skimming money from the practice to fund a gambling addiction he's had for years."

"Really?" I raised an eyebrow.

"He didn't strike me as that type of guy," Ruby said. "He seemed so...ordinary. Well, apart from the expensive car."

"He was probably playing it down when he came to see you," Vernon said. "If he did kill Pandora, he'd want it to seem like he was the shocked, estranged son. Pandora was loaded. Ian could've been in town trying to talk Pandora into giving him a loan. And when she didn't..."

"He came back and killed her to get the inheritance instead and frame Tim," I finished for him. "There's also another possible motive." I filled Vernon in about Donna, who may have been worried Pandora was out to bad-mouth Tim and ruin their business.

"We need to tell Lester all this new information," Ruby said.

"He won't listen to us," I said. "If I go back and see him, he's likely to arrest me."

"Why, what happened?" Vernon asked.

I told him about my earlier meeting with Lester and the horrible letter left on my step.

"You got a threatening note, and that asshole doesn't think it's worth investigating?" Vernon's voice rose. His face turned a similar color to Lester's. Then he winced and rubbed his belly.

"Calm down," Ruby said gently. "Stress isn't any good for stomach problems."

"But that guy's a total jerk. He makes me so angry!"

"Come on. Take a deep breath." Ruby inhaled loudly. She blew it out again with overexaggeration. "Just like that. Do it with me."

"I know how to breathe!"

"You don't. Deep breathing is designed to get some calming energy and oxygen flowing. Or how about I do a guided meditation for you to get you to relax? Or you could do the breath of fire to detoxify you."

"Breath of what? I haven't got time for all that rubbish." He waved an exasperated hand around. "I'll pop a pill instead."

He reached under the counter for one of his prescriptions and threw a couple of antacids in his mouth, swallowing them with a swig of water.

"You need to relax, darling," Ruby singsonged, her upbeat tone hiding the anxiety and worry I could clearly see in her eyes.

"I know what I'm doing," Vernon grumbled, wincing again.

"Parsley tea," Ruby said. "That's what might help. Mixed with some grapefruit seed extract and oregano oil. Full of antioxidants and natural anti-inflammatories. I'll make you some when we get home."

Vernon winced again, although I'm not sure if that was at the thought of Ruby's concoction or the pain this time. "I'd rather drink a dog-crap smoothie."

"You're such a stubborn..." Ruby struggled for the right word, her mouth flapping open and closed.

"What?" Vernon challenged her. "A stubborn what?"

"Okay, time out, you two!" I made a T sign with my hands. "You're worse than a couple of five-year-olds! I'll put you both in detention if you're not careful."

That seemed to diffuse the tension between them, and Vernon and Ruby glanced at each other, then burst out laughing.

"Can we talk about Pandora without you getting stressed?" I pointed at Vernon. "And without you worrying about Vernon?" I pointed at Ruby.

"I'm not worried. If he wants to kill himself, it's up to him." Ruby shrugged, giving her best uninterested impression, but she wasn't fooling me.

"And I'm not stressed," Vernon said.

"Then why do you look like a sweaty lobster who's about to pass out?" I put a hand on my hip and cocked my head, raising a questioning eyebrow.

Vernon sat down on a stool. "Okay, okay." He glanced at Ruby. "Look, I'm relaxing now. Satisfied?" He turned to me. "Anyway, what were you saying?"

"I was telling you how Lester is adamant that he's already got the killer. Tim's being arraigned today."

"Will he get bail pending the trial?" Ruby asked Vernon.

"I doubt it, but you never know."

"So what can we do next?" I asked.

"We need to talk to Pandora's neighbors," Vernon said. "Find out if they saw Ian near Pandora's house around the time she was killed. I've printed off a couple of photos of him from his website." Vernon headed back to the office to retrieve them and handed them to Ruby and me. I stared down at the picture. Ian was smiling, exuding confidence and compassion. But was that the smile of a cold, calculating murderer? Or was Donna involved somehow?

I glanced around the tavern. The lunch rush was over, and we'd have a few hours before the evening diners came in.

"I've got time to canvas the neighbors and visit Donna if you two can hold the fort here," I said.

"Of course," Ruby said.

"I'll come with you." Vernon took the printout from Ruby's hand.

"I thought you were resting," Ruby said.

"I did. Now I'm going to help Hope. There's no time like the present, especially if someone is threatening her. We need to get to the bottom of this before whoever wrote that note takes things one step further."

Ruby reached out and squeezed Vernon's arm. "Well, please be careful." She turned her gaze to me. "Both of you. I don't want to lose either of you guys."

* * *

I'd never set foot in Baxtor's Pharmacy before. Like Ruby and Pandora, I preferred to use natural herbal remedies if I felt ill. When I was traveling in remote places of the world, a lot of the local people used such methods, passed down from generation to generation, because it was impossible to get hold of traditional modern medicine.

Vernon stopped before we entered the shop. "It might be better for you to speak to her. She may open up more to a woman asking questions. I'll wait out here."

"Okay." I pushed open the door to the brightly lit pharmacy and grabbed the first packet of something I could see from one of the aisles before approaching the counter.

Donna stood behind it, dressed in a white lab coat over a simple gray blouse and black trousers. She looked more together today, less stressed and upset. Gone were the traces of red around her eyes. Her thick, curly hair was more tamed than when I'd seen her talking to Bud Ohlsen. She nodded sympathetically at the elderly woman in front of me who was asking advice about a carbuncle.

Donna retrieved some cream and told the woman how to apply it, before ringing it up.

"And I've got a repeat prescription I need to fill too," the woman said, handing Donna a piece of paper.

Donna examined the slip, opened a drawer behind her, and pulled out a packet of tablets, then went to a laptop at the end of the counter and typed something in. With a few clicks of her mouse, the printer behind her spewed out a label, which she stuck to the front of the box and added to the woman's purchase. Handing her the bag, she gave her a smile and told her to have a nice day.

"How can I help you?" Donna turned to me as the woman left.

I put my purchase on the counter, noticing for the first time that I'd picked up a bumper pack of condoms. Oh well, hopefully, even if I didn't get any info out of Donna, I'd still be able to put them to good use with Harvey. If we ever got to spend any time with each other without Carmen hanging around, that is.

"Just these?" Donna asked, scanning the barcode at the till, her smile still in place, although it looked tired.

I did a fake cough. "I've actually got a bit of a cough at the moment too." I did another one, just to sound believable. "Do you have anything for that?"

"Is it chesty or tickly?" Donna asked.

"Er...um..." *You see, this is the trouble with lying.* You could get muddled up in all sorts of ways, which was why I hated doing it, but I needed to stall for time while I thought of something to say. "Both?"

She turned behind her to a shelf stacked full of medicine, retrieved a bottle of cough syrup, and put it on the counter. "This is a very good brand. Should sort you out very quickly."

"Okay, great." I pulled out my wallet. "I'm sorry to hear about your husband being arrested. It must be awful for you both."

The smile slid off her face and turned into an angry scowl. "It's terrible. He's completely innocent. He was innocent all those years ago when they accused him of having something to do with Jenna's disappearance, and he's innocent now. That woman tried to ruin Tim's reputation, and now she's doing it again from beyond the grave!"

Hmmm...she didn't sound exactly sad that a woman was now dead. Was she angry enough to have killed her?

"I told Tim so many times we should get out of this place. Even though it was proven he had nothing to do with Jenna, people still hated him. Hated us. And believed all those lies that woman spouted about him. There are too many gossipers in this town."

She didn't go so far as to say she was glad Pandora was dead, but the sentiment oozed between the layers of her words.

"Did you know Pandora had called Tim that day? Trying to get him to go to her house?"

"Yes. I was here when he took the phone call." Her mouth formed into a thin, tight line. "I told him not to go there. Said nothing good could come out of it. But you know what men are like! He wouldn't listen to me, and now look what's happened." She glanced around the shop. "Business has dropped off. We've only had a few regulars in who stuck by Tim all those years ago. I used to love this town. I grew up here, it's my home, and I didn't want to be forced to move. But now I just want to get the hell out of this place and start afresh somewhere new. I've had it with all this stress."

"So you met Tim when you were both studying at the university?"

"Yes. We didn't go to the same school here, so I didn't know him that well before, but we became friends at the university."

"Did you know Jenna then, when he was seeing her?"

She shrugged. "I met her a few times around town when she was with Tim after we graduated, but I didn't really know her. Tim and I started going out with each other years after Jenna disappeared."

I thought carefully about how to word my next question, not wanting her to clam up if she suspected I was accusing her of being involved in Pandora's death. "So what happened after Tim took the phone call?"

She eyed me carefully, probably wondering if I was one of the gossipers. Then she gave a defeated shrug. "He was upset, obviously, but he said that woman told him she had some kind of evidence that proved what had really happened to Jenna. I told him not to go. I said knowing her and everything she'd done to cause trouble, it was probably some kind of trap." Her curls shook as she spat the words out. "Anyway, he ignored my advice, and he left the shop to go see her. He said he had to clear his name. When he came back, he was all flustered and upset and angry, but he wouldn't really tell me what had happened, just that they'd had some kind of argument—the same old thing, raking up the past—and he'd left. I was very tempted to go round and see her myself and tell her to stop meddling in our lives and spreading rumors about my husband."

"So then what happened?"

"Well, the next thing I knew was that Tim had been arrested for Pandora's murder while I was out the following morning taking our dog for a walk. And—" Then she burst into tears. She put her hands over her face, shoulders heaving with sobs. "There's no way he would've killed Pandora." She wiped her tears away with determined strokes of her fingers and stood up straighter. "I know what people probably thought when I married him. But it was proven he had nothing to do with Jenna's disappearance. He was completely innocent, and I believed him. He's not perfect, my husband, far from it, but he couldn't kill anyone. I just want everyone to leave us alone."

I was about to ask her another question, but she rounded the counter then and walked toward the *Open* sign hanging on the door, turning it to *Closed*.

"I'm shutting up for the day now." She held the door open for me. "I've had enough of all this."

I looked into her moist eyes and saw a deep weariness behind her glasses. "I'm really sorry for upsetting you. This must be so stressful."

She nodded and sniffed.

I said good-bye, and she closed the door behind me. I slid into the passenger seat of Vernon's car and told him what she'd said.

"She's obviously angry and upset, understandably. It must've been tough to be the wife of someone accused of murder all those years ago. And now it's starting all over again. She wants to leave town."

"Yeah, but is that because she's guilty herself?"

"I don't know. She said Tim left her in the shop that afternoon and went to Pandora's. She's got a laptop there that prints off labels for the prescriptions they sell. Is there anyway your contact can hack into it and find out if she sold any drugs at the time Pandora was killed? That would prove she was in the shop at the time."

"Or not."

"Exactly."

He whipped out his cell and spoke to his contact, telling him exactly what he needed.

* * *

There were about twenty houses on Pandora's street, and they all looked pretty similar in appearance. I took the ones on the same side of the road as Pandora's house, and Vernon took the opposite side. I started at one end, walking up the path of a home painted in a sunny lemon yellow. The door was opened a couple of inches by an elderly woman whose permed gray hair perched on top of her head like a bowl of crispy-fried noodles.

"Oh, hi, my name's Hope Foster, and I was wondering if I could ask you a quick question."

"I'm not buying anything." She suspiciously peered one eye through the small gap.

"I'm a friend of Pandora Williams." Ooops, another lie. *Sorry, Universe!* "And I'm trying to find out what really happened to her."

Her eyes narrowed further. "I thought the police got that Tim Baxtor for it."

"Yes, they did, but I'm not sure they're right."

"Course they're right. They're the police. They wouldn't arrest the wrong person, would they?"

I thought back to when they arrested me for Bob's murder. "Actually, yes, they could."

"Hmmm," she muttered in a disbelieving tone. "What do you want, then? I've got a carrot cake in the oven I need to get back to."

"Do you remember seeing this man hanging around Pandora's house recently?" I showed her the photo.

"This is her son, Ian, isn't it?"

"Yes."

"As far as I know, they haven't seen each other in years. Not that Pandora and I chatted much. She was a bit of a recluse, you know. I haven't seen her out for a long time."

"I know. So you haven't seen Ian here lately?"

"No."

"How about a woman?" I thought about Donna. "With long, curly dark hair and glasses? Did you see anyone like that hanging around on the day Pandora was killed?"

"No. And if I were you, I'd leave things to the police. They know what they're doing." She closed the door in my face.

I went to the next house. A young mom in her early twenties answered, carrying a baby on her hip. I introduced myself again.

"Oh, it's terrible what happened." She gasped, clutching the baby closer to her and smoothing his downy hair. "I thought this was a nice, quiet street, but now we're thinking about moving. Still, they got the guy, I suppose, so it's not likely he's going to come back, is it?"

"I'm not sure they have the right guy."

She gasped again, eyes wide. "Oh!"

I showed her the photo of Ian. "Do you remember seeing this man visiting Pandora recently? He's her son, Ian."

She nodded. "Actually, yes, I do remember. I was taking this little one to the clinic for his checkup." She kissed her son's head. "I was walking down the road with the stroller, and I saw that guy getting out of one of those flashy SUVs. It was..." She scrunched her face up, thinking. "A Range Rover! That's it. I know because it's my husband's dream car." She grinned affectionately. "It was red."

My heart rate kicked up a notch. "And then what happened?"

"I saw him knock on Pandora's door."

"Did you see him go inside?"

"No, I was late for the appointment, so I was rushing. You know what it's like when you've got little ones. It takes you about an hour to even get out of the house! Anyway, his car was gone when I got back about an hour later."

"And when exactly was this?"

"Um...his appointment was Tuesday at 11:30, so it would've been about 11:15."

"Did you see him again? The day after, when Pandora was killed?"

She shook her head. "No. I wasn't in that day." She stared at the photo in my hand warily. "You don't think he'll come back, do you?"

"No. I don't think so. Did you see anyone else hanging around recently? A dark-haired woman with glasses, perhaps?"

"Er...no, I don't think so."

"Thanks very much for your help."

"You're welcome."

She shut the door, and I heard a lock turn and a bolt engage behind it.

The next house was home to a retired couple who'd been out of town for a couple of days during the Labor Day holiday, so they hadn't noticed Ian or anyone else in the neighborhood. And there was no answer from the next. I made a note of the number so we could revisit at a later date if we needed to. Then I came to Pandora's immediate neighbor on her left.

The door was opened by a stout woman wearing a long flowing caftan dress in a myriad of bright colors, probably in her late sixties. Her hair was silvery blonde, braided over one shoulder.

I went through my spiel again.

Her hand went to her throat. "Oh, it's so awful what happened to Pandora. Poor, poor lady. She didn't have a happy life. What with Jenna disappearing, and then losing touch with Ian. She hardly went out of the house." She leaned forward a little closer. "It's true what they say that money can't buy you happiness. Why don't you come in, dear, and we can chat?"

"Thanks." I followed her through the hallway into a kitchen at the rear that looked the exact same layout as Pandora's but was far more modern and updated.

"Have a seat. You must have tea and something to eat." She clapped her hands together. "I don't get nearly enough visitors these days, and I've got a new quiche recipe I just worked up that I've been dying to try out on someone." She hobbled to the kettle and flicked it on before I could refuse. "I'm Lillian, by the way."

I walked closer to the patio door and glanced out into her garden. It was home to an array of planters, bushes, and trees, with an abundance of color, which was obviously immaculately cared for. In front of me was a five-foot fence identical to Pandora's that separated Lillian's property from the wooded area at the rear. I looked over to my right. From here I could see the second story of Pandora's house and the six-foot boundary fence. Lillian clattered around in the kitchen behind me.

"You must have tea in a proper teapot," she said to me. "All of these convenience tea bags just don't taste the same. Is Earl Grey okay?"

"That would be lovely, thanks."

She carried a china teapot to the kitchen table, then collected some matching china cups from the cupboard. "Have a seat."

"Thank you. This is very kind of you."

"Not at all. It's nice to have some young company. The quiche won't be long." She brought a jug of milk and a sugar bowl to the table and sat down, patting the chair next to her.

I followed suit and handed her the photo of Ian. "This is Ian, Pandora's son. Do you remember seeing him visiting with her lately?"

She took the photo from me and eyed it with a sad expression before handing it back. "I remember Ian. And Jenna, of course." She poured steaming liquid through a strainer into each delicate cup. "Pandora moved in next door just after me. We were great friends when our children were younger. Our kids were the same age and used to have playdates with each other. And we were both into holistic treatments too. Way before it got more acceptable. Pandora trained as a nurse, you know, before discovering more natural therapies and turning to that. We both used to go to the Mind, Body, and Soul conference in New York together each year. Then, of course, Jenna disappeared, and everything changed. She never really left the house after that, and she didn't like having visitors. I'd say hello to her if I saw her outside, but she didn't like to engage in conversation anymore." She took a sip of her tea. "I couldn't imagine losing my daughter like that and just not knowing what had happened."

"But Pandora was convinced Tim Baxtor killed her?"

"Oh, yes. Jenna was going to break up with him, and he was obsessed with her."

"Do you think Tim killed Jenna, too?"

"Yes. Jenna and Pandora were very close. Jenna never went through that rebellious stage that most kids go through. They were more like sisters than mother and daughter." She took another sip of tea and leaned closer. "There's no way Jenna would've just left home without telling Pandora about it." She shook her head adamantly. "No way. I'm positive of it."

"It must've been a terrible time for everyone."

"Terrible," she repeated. "So many people were looking for her. The whole town couldn't believe it could happen. Pandora had a kind of breakdown, understandably, really."

"I heard she publicly accused Tim Baxtor of having something to do with Jenna's disappearance, but there was no evidence."

"Yes. That lovely Detective Ohlsen investigated, but he couldn't find anything helpful. It was like Jenna just disappeared into a puff of smoke." She fiddled with the ends of her braid. "Anyway, Pandora never got over it. Her relationship with Ian became strained. I felt a bit sorry for him, if I'm honest. How could he ever live up to the shadow of Jenna when Pandora couldn't stop thinking about her?"

"And how did Ian and Pandora get along before Jenna went missing?" I thought about what Jenna's best friend, Melanie, had told me.

She hesitated for a moment, staring into her teacup. "Ian wasn't planned. There was a six-year age gap between him and Jenna, and reading between the lines, I think Pandora was happy with one child. She always wanted a girl, and, like I said, Jenna and Pandora both doted on one another. Pandora never seemed to bond with Ian, and I always got the feeling that he was left out a bit. Sometimes, I guess it's hard not to have favorites with your children. When her husband, Alan, was alive, it wasn't so obvious. Alan would take Ian out fishing and playing sports and so on, while Pandora took Jenna to dance and watched her cheerleading practices. When Alan died, Ian was lost, and...well, I don't think he ever got Pandora's full attention."

A timer in the shape of an apple sounded. Lillian retrieved the quiche from the oven, which wafted delicious aromas all over the kitchen, before putting it on the side to cool. "I know this sounds horrible," she said, sitting down again, "but I don't think Pandora really knew what to do with a little boy. All she ever wanted was a girl."

"So Ian left home after Jenna disappeared?"

"Yes. After about a year, he left for the university in Seattle. I don't think they kept in touch after that. Which is strange because he did visit her the day before she was..." She fanned her face with a horrified look. "The day before she was *murdered!*"

I leaned forward. "You saw him?"

"Oh, yes. It was in the morning. I was just getting the post from my box outside and saw him park there in some big red car. I couldn't believe it after all this time. He hadn't changed that much, really, just got a bit taller, so I recognized him right away. But I hoped that they were going to repair their relationship. It's never too late, is it? And when you start getting older, you think about mending burned bridges and getting back in touch with loved ones you've lost contact with."

I nodded, encouraging her to continue.

She stood up and got a couple of plates from the cupboard and a couple of forks from the drawer, closing it with her hip. She sliced two hefty chunks of quiche and brought the laden plates back to the table. "Go on. Taste it, and tell me what you think." She looked at me with excited expectation.

I took a bite and went to quiche heaven. "Delicious."

She gave a pleased nod, took a bite of her own, and chewed with a thoughtful look. "Hmmm, maybe a little more paprika and garlic next time." Resting her fork on the plate, she said, "Anyway, where was I?"

"You said you saw Ian."

"Oh, yes. I was reading the newspaper in my lounge and glanced out of the window about half an hour later, and his car was gone, so I'm not sure if they managed to sort anything out between them in that short space of time. I hope so. You don't want to go taking your disputes to the grave, do you?"

"Did you see him come back the next day at all?" I took another bite.

"No. But I did hear an argument between Pandora and Tim Baxtor."

"Really?" I nearly choked as I sucked in the mouthful of quiche. I coughed, eyes watering. I took a sip of tea to swallow away the remaining crumbs lodged in my throat.

"Yes. I was in my garden, trying to get rid of the whitefly on my rhododendrons. They've been terrible this year. Her kitchen door must've been open at the time, because I heard some of their conversation quite clearly, although Pandora was slurring her words a lot and sounded very drunk."

"What were they arguing about?"

She closed her eyes, as if reliving the memory. "Well, Pandora said she knew he'd killed Jenna and she wanted him to finally admit it to her so she could rest in peace. She wanted him to tell her what he'd done with Jenna's remains so she could have a proper burial. Then Tim called her crazy and denied having anything to do with Jenna's disappearance."

"Did Pandora mention having found any evidence that Tim had actually murdered her?"

"Not that I could hear." Lillian opened her eyes. "She just kept pleading with him to tell her what had happened to her daughter, and he kept saying she was wrong and to leave him alone, or he'd get his lawyer onto her again." She nodded conspiratorially. "But I think Tim Baxtor did kill Jenna and got away with it."

I thought about how awful it must be to think your daughter's killer was not only walking around free and living his life to the full, but doing it right in front of you in the same town. "Why didn't Pandora move away? It must've been hell for her knowing Tim was still in town."

"She couldn't, dear. Even though she believed Tim did kill Jenna, there was still that little sliver of hope that she was wrong. She couldn't move in case Jenna ever did come back."

I thought about the bedroom of a young woman, which was left exactly the same as when Jenna had disappeared. I thought about the longing Pandora must've felt. I could picture her sitting on Jenna's bed, surrounded by her things, picking up the photos of her and staring into eyes that were full of life, sobbing her heart out, desperately wanting to find out the truth.

"What else did you hear between Tim and Pandora?" I asked.

"Nothing much, really. He told her to leave him alone, and then everything went quiet. I assumed he'd left, but I didn't see him go. Then, of course, I heard about the awful news. He must've become so angry he killed her to shut her up once and for all."

"If you were in the garden, did you see or hear anyone else? Perhaps someone climbing over her rear fence?"

"No. I came inside after it got quiet, because I was going to go and check up on Pandora. Make sure she was okay. I hesitated awhile because we hadn't really spoken in years. Like I said, she was a recluse. And she was a very private person. So...I was worried about being rebuffed, really, and I suppose I hesitated a bit too long. I keep wondering what would've happened if I'd marched over there right away. Could I have saved her? It's something that will haunt me."

"I feel the same," I said sadly.

"I was just opening the front door when I saw you and Ruby Fournier approaching Pandora's front door. I guessed you had an appointment with her, so I thought everything must be okay. It wasn't until I saw the ambulance and police arrive that I found out what had happened." She wiped away a tear that sprang into her eye. "Awful, awful business. And Pandora never did find out what happened to Jenna."

"Did you see anyone else suspicious near Pandora's house? A brunette with long hair and glasses, perhaps?"

"No, I didn't, dear, just Tim and Ian, like I said."

"Did you know Pandora was ill?"

"Ill? No, she never said anything to me, but then why would she?" She made a hopeless sighing sound. "I just wish she would've let me help her." She sniffed and reached for a box of tissues on the table.

"Did you tell the police about Ian turning up and the argument you overheard with Pandora and Tim?"

"Yes. I got the impression that the argument I told them about, and the fact that you and Ruby saw Tim leaving that day, was what made them arrest Tim."

I thanked her and carried on down the rest of the street, but none of the other neighbors had witnessed anything useful. I waited by Vernon's car for him to return so we could swap information. He was on the phone as he approached me. He leaned on the hood of the car, speaking quietly before he hung up.

"That was my contact. The computer system at Baxtor's Pharmacy is linked to a central medical wholesaler's system. Apparently, when they fill a prescription, it automatically places an order for a replacement, so they never have to bother with reordering. At 3:59 p.m. on the day Pandora was killed, someone using Donna's log-in password filled a prescription for Augmentin, so she must've been in the shop, just like she said."

"We can strike Donna off as a possible suspect, then." I told him what I'd discovered from the neighbors I spoke to. Vernon had found a couple who'd also spotted Tim Baxtor leaving Pandora's when Ruby and I turned up, but no one who'd noticed anyone else suspicious hanging around.

"We should check out the rear of Pandora's property," Vernon said. "If Ian did climb Pandora's fence after Tim left, he may have dropped some incriminating evidence."

We walked to the end of the street and swung a left down a small pathway under a canopy of trees. We made our way through a clearing, counting the houses we passed, stopping outside Pandora's back fence. In between the trees and her fence was an area of short scrub, the ground covered in a carpet of decaying leaves. We wandered along the fence, gazes peeled to the floor, coming across a few rusting Coke cans, an empty water bottle, and a plastic bag that had wrapped itself around one of the tree trunks.

And there, partially sticking out of a bed of leaves, was a cheap black cell phone.

CHAPTER FIFTEEN

———

I bent down to look at it, but Vernon grabbed my arm.

"Don't touch it. We need to phone Detective Dick Head and let him know. I've got some latex gloves in the car. I'll go get them. I want to make sure this is the same phone that was used to call Tim Baxtor."

"It's got to be. It can't be coincidence that it's lying here."

"I agree, but we need to be sure." Vernon limped back to his car while I whipped out my own phone and called Lester, but he wasn't answering. He was probably too busy texting someone. I left a message, telling him what we'd found and that we were waiting at the scene.

"I wonder whose prints are on that phone," I said to Vernon as he slapped on the gloves and picked it up.

He turned the phone on and scrolled through the phone's menu. There was only one call listed on the log, and it was at 12:02 p.m. on the day Pandora was murdered. I punched in the number on my own phone and waited for it to connect. Tim Baxtor's voice mail kicked in as I held my phone between us, both listening.

Vernon studied the area carefully. The phone was a yard away from Pandora's fence. "I'm guessing either Ian called Tim to lure him here so he could frame him, probably using some kind of voice software to alter his voice and pretend he was Pandora. Then Ian dropped it after killing Pandora and escaping into the woods. Or Tim threw it over the fence from Pandora's garden to hide the evidence that he'd really called himself from this phone so he could tell everyone Pandora phoned him and he had an excuse to be there."

"That doesn't seem likely, does it? Why throw the phone away but leave the needle and vial at the scene?"

"I admit, it doesn't sound that plausible, but if he'd just killed her, he wouldn't have been thinking straight. It's easy to make mistakes then. Or maybe he heard you pull up outside and didn't have time to hide anything else. Or it really was Pandora that called Tim and asked him to visit her." Vernon let out an angry blast of air as loud as a balloon being suddenly deflated. "Lester didn't do a very good job of investigating the scene, as usual. The crime scene team should've swept this area too. He's an idiot."

If Lester had missed the phone, what other crucial evidence had he missed too?

Vernon replaced the phone on the ground exactly where we'd found it and removed his gloves, turning them inside out and shoving them into his pocket.

Twenty minutes later, Lester Marshall appeared.

"Well, well, well." He swaggered up to meet us. "I suppose you two were just out for a cozy stroll in this area, were you?"

I bristled. If Lester had been doing his job properly, we wouldn't have needed to get involved in this whole sad mess.

"Actually, we were concerned you may have missed something." Vernon gave Lester an accusing gaze. "And it looks like we were right. This is probably the same phone Tim claims Pandora used to call him on the day she was killed." Vernon didn't let on he knew for certain it was, in case heavy-handed Lester arrested him for tampering with evidence. Anyway, as an ex-FBI agent, Vernon had far more experience than Lester. "You need to do a whole sweep of this area and see if there's any other trace left out here." Vernon waved a hand around the spot we were standing in.

"Are you telling me how to do my job?" Lester gave Vernon an ugly glare. "And what does a *retired teacher* know about crime scene work?"

"Let's just say I watch a lot of police shows."

Lester barked out a laugh. "People watch *CSI* or *Law & Order* for five minutes and think they're experts these days. I'm a highly trained professional. I know what I'm doing."

Vernon muttered something under his breath.

I didn't like to point out that maybe Lester should watch those shows, too. He might learn something useful.

"Why didn't you search this area?" Vernon asked.

Another glare from Lester. He was silent for so long I thought he'd ignore the question, but eventually he grudgingly snapped, "I didn't think it was necessary to extend the search area outside of the fence."

"Not necessary?" Vernon stared at him incredulously. "This was a murder scene. You should've been all over it!"

"We already have the suspect in custody!" Lester took a step toward Vernon and poked him in the chest. "Keep out of my investigation. *I'm* in charge here, and I don't want no *Columbo*-watching do-gooders interfering. You got that?" He poked Vernon again.

Vernon's eyes narrowed to slits. "If you poke me one more time, you'll regret it."

"Really? Whatcha gonna do about it?"

Even though Vernon was in his sixties and walked with a limp, he was still a strong, stocky guy. And his FBI training meant he could take out Lester before he even had a clue what had hit him. Yep, I'd put my bets on Vernon every time. Luckily, I didn't have to find out, as Lester squatted down then and looked at the phone, so the tension between them was diffused. He pulled his own latex gloves from his pockets and went through the call log, writing down the number in his notebook. Pulling an evidence bag from his pocket, he dropped the phone in and sealed it. Then he got his own cell phone out and dialed a number, watching us with suspicion.

"Yeah, I need some crime scene officers out to Pandora Williams's place. We need to do a full sweep of the area behind her property," Lester said into the handset, as if it were all his idea.

I caught Vernon's gaze. Vernon shook his head and looked as if he wanted to do Lester an injury.

Lester hung up and treated us to another glare. I bet he sat at home practicing it in the mirror to try to look intimidating.

"Well, this just proves that Tim Baxtor is the murderer," Lester said to us.

Killer Colada | 127

"How?" A confused frown spread across my face. "Someone else could've phoned Tim to lure him to Pandora's house. Someone who climbed the fence and slipped in through the kitchen door to kill her. They could've dropped this phone when they left the same way. Did you know there's software that can disguise a voice? Whoever called Tim could've used that to *pretend* they were Pandora so Tim was framed for her death. That person could easily have been Ian."

Lester exhaled an impatient sigh. "I think it's pretty obvious what happened."

"Really?" Vernon said. "It's not obvious to me."

"Nor me," I said, waiting for Lester to enlighten us.

Lester spoke slowly, as if he were talking to a couple of idiots. "Pandora was the one who phoned Tim and asked him to come to the house. A neighbor overheard them arguing about Jenna. He killed her in a fit of rage. Then he left through the front door, which you were witness to. No one slipped in or slipped out again. Tim did it, and I'd appreciated it if you'd leave the police work to the people who know what they're doing."

Vernon folded his arms across his chest. "So maybe you can explain something about your theory."

Lester sighed again.

"If Pandora called Tim, why is the phone on the *other* side of her property fence?"

"I don't know why. *Yet.* But I'm sure when we get the fingerprints back, they'll prove Pandora used this phone."

"And what about the pentobarbital that was stolen from the vet's?" Vernon asked.

"I'm certain Tim Baxtor stole that to try to muddy the waters and point the finger at someone else," Lester said.

"Did his prints match those found at the vet's, then?" I asked.

"No. But he obviously got someone else to act on his behalf, although he's denying that too. We've checked his wife's prints, but they don't match."

"I just spoke with Pandora's neighbor, Lillian, who saw Ian turn up at Pandora's the day before she was killed."

"So?" Lester huffed at the inquisition "That's not important. Lillian also told us she heard the argument between Tim and Pandora that obviously made him snap and murder her."

"So you're not going to compare Ian's fingerprints with the ones found at the vet's clinic to see if those ones match up?" Vernon asked.

"There's no need. Like I *keep* telling you, we've got the murderer. Now stop interfering in my investigation, or I'll have you arrested. Am I making myself clear?" He made shooing gestures with his hands. "Run along now."

Vernon and I walked slowly back to his car.

"He's an idiot," Vernon muttered.

I agreed. "I'm not convinced Tim did it. There are too many inconsistencies."

"And we owe it to Tim Baxtor to make sure an innocent man isn't sent to jail."

"So what do we do next?"

"We need to get it straight from the horse's mouth."

"Huh?"

"My contact told me Tim's arraignment was postponed because the judge is off sick. He's still in the Danger Cove jail. We need to pay him a visit and find out what he's got to say."

CHAPTER SIXTEEN

———

As we trudged up the steps of the Danger Cove police station, my heart pattered nervously in my chest. I hoped Lester would be tied up at Pandora's for the next few hours and wouldn't catch us talking to his prime suspect. It was only a few months ago that Lester Marshall had locked me in one of the cells, believing I was responsible for Bob's murder. I knew how it felt to be innocent and scared, worrying yourself stupid about being convicted of a crime you didn't commit. And if Tim was innocent, we had to get to the bottom of it to prevent a miscarriage of justice from happening. If Lester caught us interfering, he'd probably sling me into jail quicker than you could say *Innocent until proven guilty!* The thought of being arrested again and incarcerated in another cell made me shiver. But what choice did we have?

Officer Richie Faria was back on the front desk today, filling in some traffic violation paperwork with a satisfied grin on his face. We explained we wanted to visit Tim Baxtor. Richie was so overeager to do well and make detective that I was worried he might call Lester and let him know we were there, and I was pretty sure Lester would use Richie's enthusiasm to his advantage, having a pair of ears and eyes on the street. Thankfully, Richie was distracted by another person coming in to report he'd lost his wallet, and told us to wait in the seating area by the front door. A few minutes later we were led by Officer Fred Fields to the very cell I'd been in before.

"These people want to visit you. That okay?" Fred asked Tim through the bars.

Tim sat on a metal cot, back against the wall, knees drawn up to his chest. His hair was flattened to his head in places. He had a few days' worth of stubble on his face, and his eyes were red and watery. Wearing a pumpkin-orange jumpsuit, he looked nothing like the smartly dressed man I'd seen emerging from Pandora's front door on that fateful day. Tim wearily dropped his feet to the floor. "I guess."

Fred unlocked the door for us to enter. We stepped inside the cramped cell, and he locked it behind us with a loud click.

"I'll give you fifteen minutes." Fred took off back down the corridor, shiny boots squeaking on the linoleum floor.

"Who are you?" Tim glanced between Vernon and me warily.

Vernon introduced us, then said, "We're trying to find out what really happened at Pandora's house that day. It seems Lester Marshall is convinced you're guilty, but there are things that don't seem to add up."

"So...you're here to help me?"

"We're here to find out the truth," I said, giving him what I hoped was a reassuring smile.

"Oh, thank God for that," he wailed, throwing his head in his hands. His shoulders heaved up and down as he sobbed into them. He sniffed a few times. Wiped a snotty nose on his rumpled sleeve and looked us in the eyes. "My lawyer's trying to help too, but...everyone thinks I did it. I know Pandora and I had some unpleasant history, but I didn't kill her. I didn't!" he wailed. "I was framed."

"So tell us what you know," Vernon said. "What happened the day she was murdered? How did you come to be at her house?"

Tim took a shuddering deep breath and began. "I'm sure you've heard the rumors that Pandora spread about me? About how she thought I'd killed Jenna, her daughter?"

"Yes," I said.

"It's not true. None of it is true. I loved Jenna. It took me a long time to get over what happened." He shook his head softly to himself and stared at a spot above our heads, a look of anguish twisting his features. "I felt like I was the luckiest guy in the world to be with her. We were so happy together. I'd just started my pharmacy business, and I proposed to her. I was living with my parents while the business got off the ground, and I saved up for a house. We had a small engagement party and were planning our wedding. Our life together was just starting, when..." He trailed off for a moment, wiping his eyes again. "Jenna phoned me on the morning of the Independence Day celebrations and asked me to meet her at the lighthouse that night, but she never showed up. At first I wasn't worried. Jenna was always late for things, but for her not to show up at all, that just wasn't like her. I waited an hour, and then I got worried she might've been in an accident, so I rushed back to Pandora's house, but Jenna wasn't there either. Pandora and I searched for her with no luck. The next few days were terrible. The police carried out their own search with volunteers from the community. I looked everywhere I could think of too, but there was no sign of her. It was like she'd vanished."

"And she didn't take anything with her?" Vernon asked. "No clothes or passport or anything?"

"No. Nothing. Her bedroom was as she'd left it. Nothing was gone. Then the days turned into weeks and months, and she didn't come back. I know Pandora always thought she would never run away, but I believed she must have, for some reason. I was brought in for questioning by Detective Ohlsen. I know it's always the partner the police look at first, so I didn't blame him. He was only trying to find out what had happened to her, the same as we all were. They let me go, of course. But there was still no word from Jenna and no leads. And we..." He threw his head into his hands again. "We never heard from her again." His voice was muffled in between his fingers.

"I'm so sorry," I said. "It must've been a terrible time."

Tim sat up and composed himself again. "It was. But I wasn't allowed to grieve for losing Jenna, because Pandora thought I was responsible. She thought I'd...killed Jenna. How could she think that?" His eyes pleaded with us, but I didn't think he was expecting an answer, and he plowed on again. "She said Jenna was going to leave me. That she'd wanted to meet me that night to end things, but I didn't believe her. We were so happy together."

"So you weren't trying to control Jenna?" Vernon asked. "You weren't obsessed with her?"

"I was *in love* with her. Maybe I was young and a little jealous, and maybe overprotective of her, too, but I never did anything to hurt her. You have to believe me! But Pandora went to the papers, accusing me of murder. She stood outside my pharmacy every day with placards calling me a murderer. She phoned me constantly, harassing me, telling me to confess."

"That must've made you pretty angry," Vernon said.

"Not angry. I could understand why she was doing it. She was grieving like I was, but I just wanted it to stop. She turned people against me in the town. My business started to suffer. And I was heartbroken too."

"So you took out a restraining order and threatened to sue her?" I asked.

"I didn't want to do it, but I had to. I didn't have a choice. She just wouldn't stop."

"Why didn't you leave town and start again somewhere new if it was affecting your business?" Vernon asked.

Tim shrugged and stared at the floor. "At first, I wanted to stay in case...in case Jenna ever did come back. I never believed she was dead, you see. I thought she'd just run away. There was always that little bit of doubt. That little bit of hope that got me through the days. I prayed for her to be alive. And I thought one day she'd walk through the door and into my arms again. And I was innocent of having anything to do with her disappearance. If I'd left, it would've looked as if I was guilty, wouldn't it? It was tough, but eventually, a lot of people forgot about what had happened. My business was going okay, and I didn't want to start again. Then I met Donna, whose roots are here, too, and we...we were happy in Danger Cove."

My heart clenched. For Jenna. For Pandora. And for him, too, if he was telling us the truth.

"So after you threatened Pandora with a lawsuit, she stopped hounding you?" Vernon asked.

"Yes. I think Pandora had some kind of breakdown. We avoided each other around town, which was easy to do, as she became kind of a recluse. And we never spoke again until the day she called me."

"Did Ian harass you in any way?" I asked

"No."

"How did he act after Jenna disappeared?" Vernon asked.

Tim scratched his head. "Well, he helped search for her with the rest of us. He was kind of a quiet guy anyway, so he didn't say much to me when I was going out with Jenna. We didn't really hit it off, if you know what I mean. He was aloof, I guess you'd call him. I wasn't into fishing or football like he was, so we didn't really have much to talk about. I struggled to find things to say to him."

"And Jenna and Ian...how did they get on?" Vernon asked.

"Um...the same, I guess. They weren't very close."

"Did he seem jealous of his sister?" I asked. "Jealous that Jenna was his mom's favorite?"

Tim chewed on his fingernail, thinking about that. "Maybe. I remember one time that really sticks out in my mind. Jenna was about twenty, so Ian must've been fourteen. He'd won an award in a biology competition at school and wanted Pandora to go to watch the ceremony one night. But it corresponded with an exhibition the Danger Cove Art Museum was holding of local artists' work, where Jenna was exhibiting her sketches. I was having dinner with them, and Pandora told Ian she couldn't possibly go to his event, as she'd already agreed to go to Jenna's. Ian got so angry, he punched a hole in the Sheetrock wall and stormed out of the house."

So Ian had a temper. And he must've been jealous of his sister, craving his mom's affection and attention and probably not receiving much. I knew how that felt, growing up in the commune with two alcoholics who didn't even notice if I was there or not, being palmed off onto other people all the time, having to find my own amusement, my own happiness, my own sense of belonging. At times I'd been angry, frustrated, jealous, upset too, although that hadn't made me want to kill anyone. But it could've pushed Ian over the edge. As a hormonal teenage boy growing up without the father who'd been the only parent to nurture him, I could see how it could've tipped the scales. Pushed him to do something drastic in an angry heat of the moment.

Pushed him to get Jenna out of their lives so he could get his mom to finally take notice of him.

"Did Ian get angry a lot?" Vernon asked.

"I didn't see anything else, but he had it in him. He was always quite broody, you know. Like there was an inner anger just bubbling away under the surface." A sudden thought seemed to strike him then. "What, do you think Ian could've killed Jenna?"

"It's possible," I said.

"You're right." Tim sat up straighter. "I guess I'd never thought about that before because I always believed she was still alive somewhere."

"What happened after Pandora stopped hounding you?" Vernon asked.

"Well, she had the breakdown, and Ian left Danger Cove. I think he couldn't compete with his sister's memory in Pandora's eyes, and he felt neglected. He couldn't compete with her alive or dead. I haven't seen him since he left all those years ago. But if he did really kill Jenna, then he could've killed Pandora too, couldn't he?"

"It's possible. Was it definitely Pandora who called you that day and asked you to come to the house?" Vernon asked. "Think carefully."

Tim chewed on his lower lip. "I...I haven't heard her voice for nearly twenty years, so I suppose it's hard to be certain, and she was kind of hysterical and sounded drunk, slurring her words. The voice was a bit muffled, but I think it was her. Why would someone else call me and pretend to be her?"

Vernon and I glanced at each other. Even though Tim seemed forthcoming and honest in what he was saying, we couldn't give away our theory of some unknown person slipping inside Pandora's kitchen after Tim had left, in case it influenced what he told us.

"And anyway, when I got to her house, she was expecting me, so it must've been Pandora."

"She was?" I wondered if that little snippet had just bounced our theory out of the water.

"Yeah."

Vernon pursed his lips at that revelation. "What did the person on the phone say to you?"

"Like I said, she sounded drunk, but she said she wanted me to come over at half past three that afternoon because she'd discovered some kind of evidence about what had happened to Jenna. Of course, I agreed instantly. If Jenna was still alive, I wanted to know about it as soon as possible. And if she wasn't, I wanted to know who'd killed her. Donna didn't want me to go and bring up all the old history, but I wanted to clear my name once and for all. There are still a lot of people here who shun me, thinking I'm a murderer who got away with it."

"Did you know Pandora was dying of a brain tumor?" I asked.

"What?" Surprise registered on his face. "No. No, of course not. Like I said, we hadn't seen each other or spoken in years. She obviously didn't use my pharmacy for any medication."

"So what happened when you arrived at Pandora's?" Vernon asked.

"When I got there, she accused me of killing Jenna again, which was completely opposite to what she'd said on the phone. She demanded to know what I'd done with Jenna's body. I tried to calm her down. Tried to tell her she was wrong, but she was irrational and emotional. She wouldn't take any notice of what I was trying to say."

"Did she threaten you?" Vernon asked.

"No, not really. She just kept asking me to tell her where Jenna was. And then...when I knew she wouldn't listen to reason, I left." He rested his hands on his knees, leaning forward, eyes imploring. "She was alive when I went out of her house. You have to believe me."

CHAPTER SEVENTEEN

———

"Do you think he's telling the truth?" I asked Vernon as he drove us back to the tavern.

"My gut instinct is telling me yes."

"That's the impression I got too."

Which left us back with our own theory that someone else had entered Pandora's house through the rear and had then murdered her in the five minutes Ruby and I were sitting outside her house. But how could the murderer plan it so precisely to make it look like Tim had done it?

Vernon was obviously thinking the same, because he said, "Everyone knew of Tim and Pandora's history. If someone wanted to kill her and pin it on someone else, Tim would be the perfect scapegoat."

"It had to be Ian. He's the only other person with a motive."

"But we're just left with more unanswered questions. How could Ian have known Tim would be there if it was Pandora who made the call? And it sounds like it was, by all accounts. I'll get my contact at Seattle PD to call me as soon as they've analyzed the cell we found for prints, but let's assume she did call Tim."

"Ian was seen in the area the day before Pandora died. Maybe he was watching her. Watching the house. Waiting for an opportunity to do it. Maybe it was just lucky for him that Tim was there that day. He could've been intending to kill her anyway and make it look like a burglary gone wrong or something. We know he was in Danger Cove that day, because of the speeding ticket. He could've parked the car somewhere, approached on foot from the rear, using the cover of the woods, then when he saw or heard Tim inside the house, he was offered the perfect opportunity to frame him."

"Maybe. But what about the pentobarbital that was stolen from Adam Whittaker's vet clinic?"

"Neither Tim nor Ian would need to steal it since they could easily pilfer it from their own businesses. And it's too much of a coincidence that the very drug used to kill Pandora was stolen a few weeks before."

"Lester could be right about one thing. It could be a red herring, designed to throw people off the scent from finding the truth and make it point to a random killer."

"Ian must've stolen it to point the finger at someone else if he was ever arrested." Vernon tapped the steering wheel thoughtfully. "If Lester won't compare Ian's prints with the ones left from the vet's, we'll just have to try to find some other evidence that proves it."

When we arrived at the tavern's parking lot, I spotted Harvey in his rental vehicle.

He jumped out of it with a bouquet of stunning red flowers in his hand. "Wow, nice hair! It looks gorgeous."

Before I could say thanks, Vernon patted his gray hair. "Thanks. Are those for me?" He grinned at Harvey. "You shouldn't have. People will talk." He pressed a hand to his chest in an overdramatic way and fluttered his eyelashes.

I elbowed Vernon and laughed.

Harvey laughed back, then shuffled from foot to foot, cheeks flushing. "Um...well...actually..."

Vernon chuckled again. "I'll leave you guys to it." He limped into the tavern, leaving us alone.

"They're for you." Harvey held out the flowers. "To say sorry for breaking our date tonight. And for neglecting you lately."

I took them, my smile widening. I sniffed the spray of lush red amaryllis. "They're gorgeous. Do you know what they mean?" I'd always loved nature, and when I'd been volunteering at a women's empowerment project in India, I'd met a local woman who knew all about the ancient and mystical meanings of various flowers.

"Um...no. But they looked nice."

"According to an old legend, the woman this flower is named after was shy and timid, and fell in love with a guy called Alteo, but her love was unrequited."

"Really? What happened?"

"Apparently, she tried to win him over by giving him something he wanted most."

"Oh yeah?" He gave me a sly grin. "And what would that be?"

"Not that!" I playfully swatted his arm. "No, it was a unique flower. One that had never existed before. So she consulted an oracle, and he told her to dress in white and appear at Alteo's door every night for thirty nights."

"That doesn't sound so bad."

"Yeah, but she had to pierce her heart every night with a golden arrow."

Harvey winced. "Ouch. That's a little extreme."

"Big ouch, because when Alteo finally opened his door to her, all he found was a red flower, which had been made from the blood of Amaryllis's heart."

"Pretty tragic."

I nodded, sniffing the flowers again, wondering if it was a sign from the Universe. Was Carmen Amaryllis? Appearing at Harvey's door late at night dressed in white, her love unrequited? Or was I?

"George, the guy in the flower shop, never mentioned all that." Harvey pulled me toward him, and I molded to his warm, firm body. God, I'd missed him lately. "I really am sorry I've been so busy. I've only got a few spare minutes before I need to go back to Seattle and document the piece of hull I found."

"You must be so excited." I pulled back, staring into his sea-blue eyes, wishing I could stay there and drown in them forever. "Carmen told me."

"Yes. First the bell and now a section of the hull. With any luck we'll find more soon. This is the bee's knees!"

"The bee's what?"

"Bee's knees. I guess you'd say amazing or awesome."

"Oh, right." I laughed. "You Brits have some really weird sayings."

"What, and you Americans don't? I still can't get over the whole fanny thing."

"Huh?"

"You call an arse a fanny, right?"

"No, a butt!"

"See, this is what I'm talking about." He chuckled. "A fanny is a..." He wiggled his eyebrows suggestively.

"A what?"

"Your bits and bobs."

"*What*? Bits and bobs? Omigod, you crack me up. I don't have a clue what you're talking about.

"You *know*. Your lady bits."

I slapped a hand to my forehead. "Seriously?"

"Yeah."

"So if I said I had a fanny pack, that'd make you laugh, right?" I grinned.

He threw his head back with laughter, slapping his knee. "Hilarious!"

"What about if I fell on my fanny?" I smirked

"Well, I'd say I hope you didn't break it." He raised a suggestive eyebrow, then glanced at his watch. "Oh, bum, I have to go."

"Bum? That's like a Brit version of fanny, right?" I laughed again.

"Yeah, I think we could be here all day at this rate." He grinned, but the humor sparkling in his eyes died away as they searched mine. There was something serious in them now, something I couldn't read. He paused for a moment, taking hold of my hand not grasping the bouquet. "Look...about Carmen..." He paused, looking away shyly.

My heart clenched in anticipation of what he was going to say. That he and Carmen were getting back together? That he still loved her? That they were much better suited because they did the same job? Spoke the same language?

"Yoo-hoo!" A familiar voice shouted behind me.

Talk of the devil.

Carmen strode toward us, looking stunning, as always. "I thought I heard your voice." She beamed at Harvey and glanced at the bouquet I was holding. "Oh, are they for the funeral of that woman who was killed?" She pulled a sad face, which, like most of Carmen, seemed fake. Before I could correct her, she said to Harvey, "How did you get on? You haven't finished cataloguing everything already, have you?"

"No, I just popped back to speak to Hope. I'm headed back there soon."

She touched Harvey's arm and let her hand linger there. "While you're here, I've just found something *very* interesting I want you to take a look at." She had an excited gleam in her eye. "Come on." She gently took Harvey's hand and led him away.

Harvey glanced at me as she propelled him forward. He mouthed the words *I'll give you a bell.*

Which in Harvey's language meant he'd call me.

I watched them go, a nervous knot curling up in my stomach as Carmen's hand still clutched Harvey's, disappointment and jealousy welling up inside. What had he been about to say?

I stomped into the tavern, head down to avoid spotting them looking all cozy together outside the garden area.

"Nice flowers!" Ruby said from behind the bar as I swung open the door.

"Hmph," I said, sniffing them again. They were beautiful. And so was Carmen.

Argh! Go away, negative thoughts!

"What does that mean?" she asked.

"It's obvious Carmen's after Harvey. And it seems like we're drifting apart, and..." I slumped down on the stool, leaned my elbows on the bar, and rested my chin in my hands, staring at an ancient scratch in the wood. *And I'm in love with him? And I'm worried about getting my heart broken again? And...*

Ruby enveloped me in a hug. "You know, not everyone in this world is going to like you. Some people are meant to come into your life as a reminder to watch the company you keep. Everything we go through is a lesson. There's something to learn from every situation. And the lesson here is that if you focus on your enemies and your weaknesses, you'll be defeated by them." She rubbed a comforting hand up my back.

I nodded into her shoulder. Hadn't the tarot cards said something similar? "Yes. You're right."

"I always am." She chuckled.

"No you're not. You just think you are," Vernon muttered as he rounded the bar. "And you're especially *not* right about thinking a tofu omelet tastes anything at all like eggs! That's what she was feeding me for breakfast this morning. It's gross!"

"Blah, blah, blah," Ruby muttered. "It was so gross you wolfed it down and left nothing on your plate." She let go of me. "Anyway, Moaning Minnie here has been filling me in regarding your sleuthing." She jerked her head in Vernon's direction.

"Yes," I said, grateful I had something to concentrate on other than Harvey and Carmen.

"So you really think Ian did it?" She shook her head. "If he is guilty, it puts me in an awkward position now. I've finalized the arrangements for Pandora's funeral this morning while you were out, and I was going to phone him and let him know, but now I feel a bit...well, awkward."

"I can call him for you and let him know what's happening," Vernon suggested. "We don't want to let it slip we think he's a suspect at this stage."

"Would you? Thanks." She exhaled a relieved breath. "It must be terrible for Tim, being accused of murder for the second time, if he really is innocent."

I thought about Jenna again. How she'd just vanished without a trace. Everyone had said Jenna wouldn't have left without saying good-bye to Pandora, so something bad must've happened to her, and I definitely believed now she was dead. But if Tim hadn't killed her, Ian was definitely looking like the favorite. I'd been convinced Jenna's disappearance had something to do with Pandora's death. But what? And how? After all this time, with a cold trail and no evidence, I guessed the only way we'd find out would be if Jenna's body was finally discovered, and that looked desperately unlikely after twenty years.

CHAPTER EIGHTEEN

———

I slept badly that night, thoughts and images invading my dreams. Pandora's lifeless eyes. Tim's pleas. Ian's statement that he hadn't seen his mom in years. Harvey's dimples. Carmen's beauty. Harvey and Carmen cozying up together in their rooms at the B&B. At one stage, Carmen was floating outside Harvey's bedroom door in a long white gown, her golden hair braided, like an ethereal King Arthur's court princess. Harvey swung the door open, wearing britches, knee-high swashbuckling boots, and a white shirt with poufy long sleeves. He dragged her into his room and threw her onto the bed, all set to ravish her (not that she needed any encouragement). They were in the throes of a passionate, bodice-ripping embrace when her heart exploded, sending red flowers shooting out in all directions before raining down from the ceiling and smothering Harvey.

I awoke in a cold sweat with the early dawn light pushing through a gap in the curtains. I dislodged Zen from his usual position curled on my pillow above my head. He half opened his eyes as if to berate me for disturbing his twenty-two out of twenty-four hours sleep a day. Then he gave a little snore and rolled on his back. Karma was at the end of the bed, twitching, lost in his own dream. I hoped it was better than mine.

I downed a glass of hot water with fresh lemon, staring out at the sunrise edging up over the sea. Then I did a half-hour revitalizing yoga flow, to get rid of my negative energy, and meditated for ten minutes, trying to stop Harvey's and Carmen's faces appearing. After munching down some organic granola with soy milk, I was feeling ready to start the day.

Zen shot out of the bedroom, suddenly wide awake and having a freaky five minutes, scampering across the floor, climbing up curtains, and chasing his tail. Then he flew down the steps to the external door, meowing outside the kitty flap, unwilling to let himself out.

"You can get out yourself, you know," I groaned, but still opened the door for my lazy cat. He leaped through the door like a cat out of hell, and that's when I noticed the envelope on the doorstep.

Somehow I doubted it was a letter from the Good Food Awards letting me know the tavern had won a prize for its culinary delights, because it was exactly the same MO as before. Plain white envelope with my name on it, those familiar blocky letters in bold black pen. I rushed back upstairs to find some rubber gloves that I used for cleaning, donning them and rushing back.

Gingerly, I opened the envelope's flap, wondering if whoever had sent the letter had licked it. Could the police get DNA from saliva? Would Lester even bother checking? Fat chance!

I WARNED YOU! BACK OFF, OR ELSE...

Or else what? I wanted to shout from the doorway into the dawn air, but whoever had left it there was probably long gone now. After locking up the external door again, I walked through to the tavern from the internal staircase and corridor. Flipping the lights on, I tried to forget about the threats and concentrate on getting the place ready to open. I still had hours before I opened up, and my gaze kept straying to the note I'd left on the bar top, ready to take to Lester.

Did this mean we were getting close to finding out who killed Pandora? If it was from Ian, how did he know we suspected him? Was he watching me right now? I peeked out of the window, just to check if anyone was out there, and noticed Carmen, who was already busy working. Whatever Carmen had discovered yesterday must've been interesting if she was back on site at this time in the morning. Had she found more gold coins?

I watched her long, lithe limbs stride across the cliffs as she carried a large plastic box to the storage barn at the back of the tavern, which Harvey had been using to keep his tools in.

Then she returned and disappeared behind the privacy tent. A rush of emotions swirled inside. Were those the last flowers Harvey would buy me? Were they some kind of good-bye? Had he slept with her?

My phone let out a relaxing waterfall chime, the ringtone for a text message, and I retrieved it from my bag. It was from Vernon, letting me know his contact had found out that the only fingerprints found on the cell phone we'd discovered were from Pandora.

I switched on the coffee machines and boiled the kettle, making a cup of chamomile tea. Dunking the tea bag in the steamy water, I wondered what that meant. If Pandora had definitely made the call to Tim, asking him to go to her house, why had the phone ended up on the other side of her boundary fence, where it led to the woods? The only logical conclusion I could come up with was that she'd thrown it over the fence herself because she was scared of any repercussions from Tim once she'd lured him there. He'd had her arrested in the past for harassment, and she was probably worried he might try to sue her again.

I unlocked the front door to the tavern and sat outside in the pub garden with my back toward the area Carmen was working in, staring out at the sea and sipping my tea. It was a deep blue today. As smooth as a sheet of glass. Perfect conditions for Harvey to continue his search for the rest of the *Ocean's Revenge*.

I shook my head to steer the thoughts away from Harvey and back to Pandora. I still thought Tim was telling the truth, and some things began clicking into place now. Pandora was dying of an inoperable tumor and probably thought this would be her final chance to discover the truth about Jenna, so she called Tim on the pretense that she had discovered some kind of evidence about Jenna to get him to her house. He was hoping to clear his name. Otherwise he would never have gone near the place. But when Tim arrived, she gave him one last desperate plea so she could get the answers before she left this world, hoping to put Jenna to rest finally. They argued about things. Then Tim left. And in the five minutes we were waiting outside, Ian sneaked in the rear door to the kitchen, killed Pandora for her inheritance, and then vanished without being seen. Just like Jenna had done all those years ago.

Ian had obviously lied when he said he hadn't been to Danger Cove or seen Pandora recently. He was spotted the day before, when I suspected he must've asked his mom for a loan to save his flagging business or fund the gambling lifestyle he was used to. And when she refused, he returned the next day, killed her, and sped out of town, getting a traffic ticket in the process. So how did we prove Ian was actually at Pandora's that day, when no one had spotted him nearby?

I didn't have a clue. It was like searching for a ghost, just like Jenna.

I was so deep in thought that I didn't hear the gate into the garden opening from behind me. It was only Harvey putting a hand on my shoulder, which made me jump into the here and now.

My heart pounded in my chest, my sudden surprise giving way to something that made me warm and melty all over.

"Hi!" I smiled. "You scared me."

"Sorry." He sat down opposite me, making the bench bounce under his weight. "You were miles away."

I stared into his gorgeous eyes. Eyes that were creasing at the corners with a warm smile. He took my hands in his and rubbed my palms with his calloused fingers.

"Where were you?" he asked.

"Huh? When?"

He gave me a boyish, lazy grin, and the dimple came out to greet me. "Just now. What were you thinking about?"

"Oh, right. Um…I was just trying to make sense of what happened to Pandora." I told him what we'd discovered so far.

"Crikey."

"How about you? What's going on with the recovery?" I glanced over my shoulder at Carmen, who was standing up now, stretching her arms above her head and watching us.

Harvey's brow crinkled. "Carmen found something odd yesterday."

"Odd how?"

"You know I recovered the gold and silver coins from the caves underneath here? And Carmen's taken over recovering the skeletons of what we suspect to be some of the smugglers who were trapped inside when the entrance collapsed?"

I nodded.

"Well, she found a piece of silver, but it's not that old and can't be part of the smugglers' haul from 1852, because it has a modern hallmark on it. We're not quite sure how it came to be in the earth around the cave entrance."

"How old is it?"

"I took it to the university to get a second opinion, and they agreed with my estimate. We think it's only about thirty years old."

"Maybe someone dropped it, and it worked its way into the soil over the years. Is it a coin, too, like the others you recovered?"

"No." He pulled a small, sealed plastic bag out of his pocket. "It's a pair of earrings." He handed it to me.

The breath drained from my throat as I stared at them, turning the bag over so I could examine them from every angle to be sure. They were about an inch long, with a little silver feather dangling from the end of each one. And I'd seen something exactly like them before. When I was clearing Jenna's room, I'd found a matching charm bracelet with lots of little feathers on it. These earrings had to have been part of a set. But how did they end up underground? Had Jenna lost them at some point before she disappeared? Had she been to the tavern one day, and they'd fallen out? I could understand accidentally losing one earring, but two? It was unlikely but not impossible. So either she'd lost them here or...

And then a horrible picture tumbled into my head, and I thought I knew.

CHAPTER NINETEEN

———

"I'm pretty sure these belonged to Jenna," I gasped.

"The missing Jenna?"

"Yeah."

"So how did they end up there?" Harvey glanced over to the dig site, a pensive expression on his face.

I swallowed down the lump in my throat. "Either she lost them, or she..." I licked my dry lips. "Or she could've been buried with them." My gaze turned to where his was resting.

"Oh bugger."

"Are you sure all the bones you've discovered so far in the cave are all from the 1850s?"

"Yes, they're definitely bones of antiquity."

I leaped to my feet. "I need to make sure these earrings match the bracelet I found in Jenna's room, just to be sure. I need to go back to Pandora's and check and then—oh damn!" I slapped a hand to my forehead. "Ruby and I took everything to the thrift store! I hope they haven't sold them already. Can I take this?" I wiggled the bag at Harvey.

"Yes, of course." He stood too.

"And..." My gaze drifted back to Carmen and the site. "Maybe you should stop work there for a while. Just in case it turns out to be a crime scene."

Harvey stood and nodded vigorously. "Let me know what you find out." He leaned over and kissed my cheek before I rushed off to my get my bike.

I cycled into town, feet pedaling like a whirlwind, hair whipping up behind me. It wasn't until I arrived outside the thrift store that I realized it was still too early for them to be open. There was a closed sign on the door and the opening times written on a piece of paper. I glanced at my watch. I still had half an hour to kill.

Ooops, maybe I shouldn't say kill. An image of someone digging a shallow grave into the cliffs on my land and callously throwing Jenna's lifeless body down there blasted into my head.

I hopped back on my bike and cycled to Veggie Tables, the health food café just down the road. I could sit there and wait.

There were two occupied tables when I pushed my way inside, and no queue. I ordered a soy chai latte and an organic zucchini muffin, taking them to a table near the window. I picked at the muffin but couldn't get it down my closed-up throat. I was finding it hard to get the image of Jenna lying underneath those cliffs, rotting away, out of my head. I was sure her body was down there somewhere near to where her earrings had been found. I thought about the residents who'd been out there searching for her all those years ago, and all the time, had she really been so close by?

I put the muffin back on the plate and pushed it away, shivering and sipping at my drink to warm up.

I glanced at my watch every two minutes and texted Ruby and Vernon to let them know my latest discovery, then carried on checking my watch. Ruby was teaching a yoga class in Seattle this morning, so she probably wouldn't get my message for a few hours yet. Vernon phoned me a few minutes later.

"Are you sure they're the same earrings?" he asked.

"As sure as I can be. I'm just waiting for the thrift store to open so I can get the bracelet back and compare them."

"Do you need any help?"

"No, I got this. Maybe you could head for the tavern in case I'm not back in time to open up?"

"No problem."

"Oh, and I got another threatening note." I told him what it said.

"Are you going to give it to Lester?"

"I don't know if it's worth it. I haven't heard anything back from him about the last one, so it's not exactly a priority for him, and he's not taking the threat seriously. He probably hasn't even bothered checking it for prints."

"How about if I get my contact in Seattle to run a fingerprint check on it?"

I rubbed my forehead. "Yeah, that would probably be better, although I guess if they find any, they'd need to have a suspect or someone already in their system to compare it to."

"Well, there's no harm in trying."

"Okay. I left it on the bar."

"I'll courier it over to him and see what happens." He hung up.

Finally, it was time for the store to open, and I cycled back up the road. I haphazardly leaned my bike against the glass window and swung open the door.

I breathed a huge sigh of relief as I spotted Sarah Pohoke behind a counter in the middle of the shop. She was a sweet old lady, the wife of my lawyer, Aaron, who was handling Bob's will and had seen me through the stressful aftermath when Elise and Carter had tried to contest it. Her tiny frame was almost lost behind the large box from which she was unfolding clothes. I recognized them as some of the ones I'd got from Jenna's wardrobe. Hopefully, that meant I wasn't too late.

She glanced up at me and smiled. "Hello, dear, nice to see you again. How've you been?"

"Not too bad, thanks to everything Aaron did to help me. How are you?"

"Keeping busy, as you can see." She chuckled. "Just because I'm old doesn't mean I can't still be useful. I volunteer here three days a week. Keeps me out of trouble!"

She put the skirt she was unfolding on the counter and smoothed it out. "Are you looking for something specific? Ladies' garments are all on this side." She swept her hand toward the left side of the shop.

"Actually, I dropped off some clothes and jewelry a couple of days ago with Ruby Fournier. We were helping to clear out Pandora Williams's house? But the shop was closed, so we left it on the back step. This is some of it right here." I nodded to the bag beside her.

"Oh, yes, that's right. Thank you for that, dear. I've been getting it ready for sale." She shook her head softly. "Terrible business, that. Poor Pandora. She had an awful time over the years."

"She did. Have you sold any of it yet? It's just that there was a silver charm bracelet in there, and I urgently need to get it back."

"Oh." Her fingertips went to her lips. "What a shame. I put the jewelry out on display yesterday, and I seem to remember someone coming in and buying that bracelet. Let's check." She walked toward a glass display shelf in the middle of the ladies' section. On it were various pieces: broaches, lockets, bracelets, earrings, necklaces. "Let me see..." She glanced around the items. "No, it's not here. I must've sold it."

I did a mental foot stamp. "I don't suppose you know who bought it, do you?"

She tapped her lips, head tilted, thinking. "It was very busy yesterday. We only had a few locals in, and the rest were tourists so..." She walked back to the counter. "I'll go through the receipts and check." She reached into the till and took out a receipt pad, flicking through the handwritten carbon entries. "I always like to write out the receipts. I'm a bit stuck in the old days." She glanced up and smiled before licking her finger and shuffling pages backward, studying her handwriting.

I tapped my foot and chewed on my bottom lip.

"Ah! Here it is. Oh, yes, I remember now." She turned the receipt pad toward me. In her scrawled handwriting was an entry for one silver bracelet with feather charms. I looked at the name at the top of the page: Kelly Parker.

Three cheers for the old days! I just hoped Kelly wasn't a tourist who'd already left town.

"Do you know who this person is?" I tapped the pad next to the name. "Are they local?"

"Oh, yes, dear. Kelly lives on Fletcher Way. She's always in and out of here and the antique stores looking for unusual one-off bargains. Look for the house with the tub in the garden, and that's hers."

"A tub?"

"Yes. She's got an old claw-foot bathtub she recycled into a planter for herbs. You can't miss it."

"Great, thanks so much!"

"You're welcome. Have a nice day," she called out.

I hopped back on my bike and headed toward Kelly's house. Halfway down Fletcher Way I spotted the tub. I leaned my bike against the mailbox and hurried up the front path, a waft of mint and cilantro drifting on the breeze. I knocked and waited.

Please be in. Please be in!

The door swung open, revealing a middle-aged woman with her hair tied back in a severe ponytail, dressed in a pair of yoga pants and a tank top.

"Hi, I'm sorry to bother you," I said. "My name's Hope Foster from the Smugglers' Tavern. Sarah Pohoke from the thrift store in town said you bought a silver charm bracelet there yesterday with feathers on it?"

Kelly nodded warily. "Yes, I did. Why?"

"Well, there's been some kind of mix up," I said, still not wanting to alert anyone to the fact that Jenna could be buried out there on top of the cliffs. What if I was wrong? "I was helping Ruby Fournier clear out Pandora Williams's things after her death, and that bracelet was put in the thrift bag by mistake. I urgently need to get it back." Everyone in town knew Ruby, and I was hoping her name might lend some credence to my bizarre request.

"I was going to give it to my daughter. She loves that kind of thing." Her brow furrowed with what looked like disappointment.

"I'm so sorry about this, but I really need to get it back. It's very important."

"But it's her birthday tomorrow, and she's been looking for a bracelet like this for ages."

"The bracelet is actually an old family heirloom that her son wants to keep. It's been in the family for generations, with great sentimental value." Ooops, another teensy lie slipped out. *Sorry, Universe! Please don't let my punishment be too harsh. It's all for a good reason.* "Like I said, it was given to the thrift store by mistake. And since it was my fault, I *really, really* need to get it back." I gave her my best pleading, puppy-dog eyes.

"I bought that bracelet in good faith."

"I'll give you whatever you paid for it." I pulled my wallet out of my pocket and fumbled inside for some bills. "How much was it?"

"Twenty dollars."

I pulled out a twenty.

"But then there was the trolley fee I took in town." She eyed my wallet. "And then I stopped and had lunch at the Lobster Pot."

I glanced up at her, eyes wide.

She shrugged casually. "And then I lost my trolley ticket, so I had to buy another one. It was an expensive trip. I'd say about sixty dollars should cover it."

I blinked at her.

"What? That bracelet is a collector's item, too. Very rare, you know."

"Sixty dollars?!" I was about to say that I couldn't really be expected to pay for all that, but I needed that bracelet back, so I pulled out the money and handed it toward her. "There you go."

She took the money, holding the bills up to the light and checking them with suspicion to make sure they were genuine.

Hey, you're the one who's scamming me!

Satisfied they were okay, she said "Wait here" and shut the door behind her.

I shuffled on the step until she came back. She handed me the bracelet in a small, clear bag.

Before she could change her mind or try to get more money out of me, I whipped it away. "Thanks."

"Hey, I got a nice antique broach the other day, if you want that too?" she called out as I hurried back down the path. "It'll be a bargain for you at a hundred dollars."

"No, thanks!" I called out and hopped onto my bike, butt (or fanny) on the saddle, feet resting on the road to keep me steady while I pulled the earring bag Harvey had given me out of my pocket. I pressed them together, comparing the silver feathers.

Yes, they were definitely from the same set. The earrings must have belonged to Jenna.

CHAPTER TWENTY

―――

"I'll have to call Lester Marshall," I said to Vernon and Harvey, who were waiting for me at the entrance to the dig site when I arrived. Carmen was nowhere around. I passed the two bags to Vernon. "These earrings must've been Jenna's."

Vernon examined them and agreed, passing the bag to Harvey, saying, "It means you'll have to shut down the dig for now."

"Yep." Harvey ran a hand through his messy cropped hair.

I took out my cell phone and dialed Lester.

"Don't tell me you've found another dead body," Lester said to me, sarcasm oozing from his voice. "I'd hate to spend any time with you. I might end up with a knife in my back."

I didn't point out that if someone did stab him in the back, there would probably be a queue of suspects a mile long. "Um...not yet, but I think there could be one buried on my land."

"Really? And what makes you think that?" he drawled.

I told him about Carmen's discovery of what we believed were Jenna's earrings. "I think you need to get some crime scene people up here to check the area. If her earrings were buried underground, it's likely her body is here too."

I heard the sound of chewing on the other end, as if he was stuffing down his breakfast. "Well, I'll be the judge of that." More chewing. "Make sure that English guy doesn't start poking around down there anymore. I want all work stopped immediately. I'm just down the road in my car, so I'll be there soon."

I hung up and stared at the ground, a hollow feeling in my stomach. Vernon went to open up the tavern and left me standing with Harvey.

"Where's Carmen?" I asked.

"She's in Seattle, doing some cataloguing work of the apothecary bottles."

He turned to me. "Look, I know things have been so mad lately that we haven't got to spend much time with each other, and I'm sorry about that."

"Me too." I reached for his hand and squeezed it.

He lifted my hand, staring down at it. "And you know...Carmen. Well, what I was trying to tell you the other night was—"

"Step away from my crime scene!" Lester barked out, appearing from behind us. We turned and watched him swagger toward us, waving his hands around wildly like he was swatting at a swarm of bees.

I rolled my eyes at Harvey and then turned to Lester. "But we need to show you some things first, before you get started."

Lester's hand went to his hip. He was about to say something, when the crime scene vehicle pulled up in the car park and a couple of guys unloaded some equipment. Lester pointed at us. "Don't move an inch."

"But you just told us to step away," Harvey said. "Do you want us to move or not?"

"Not." Lester walked toward the officers, spoke to them briefly, then headed back our way with them in tow. "Now, show us exactly where you discovered the earrings and how you came to find them."

"Well, as you know, I've been recovering some ancient artifacts relating to the *Ocean's Revenge*." Harvey pointed to the entrance of the cave in the ground. "My associate and I have found several gold and silver coins and other items dating back to the 1850s, along with the skeletal remains of who we believe to be smugglers working on the ship at the time it sank."

"You've already found skeletons?" one of the crime scene guys asked.

"Yes. Everything we've already excavated is at University of Washington's research department in Seattle and has been fully catalogued there. I'm working closely with them. But what we'd found so far is consistent with bones that have been in the ground for a hundred and fifty odd years. But then yesterday, my colleague, Carmen, found this." He handed Lester the bag of earrings. "But these have a more modern hallmark. Probably only thirty years old."

"And I recognized the style from Jenna's room in Pandora's house," I said. "She'd kept all her daughter's things, and there was a matching bracelet."

Harvey handed him the second bag. "Part of the ground here has collapsed, so it's possible that the earrings were in the ground somewhere near to the hidden cave entrance and have worked their way into the cave over the years because of tree roots that used to be here."

Lester handed the bags to one of the crime scene guys, who put them both in a clear plastic bag and sealed them. "Right." He pointed at Harvey. "You can wait here for a while in case we need to question you about anything else you've been doing on site." He jerked a thumb at me. "And you can go and do whatever it is you do when you're not discovering dead bodies."

I left them to it and busied myself in the bar to avoid looking out of the window at what they were doing. Was Jenna really out there? Part of me hoped she was. At least that way there would finally be some kind of closure. But it would come too late for Pandora. And the only one left to mourn her was Ian, who could be a murderer, too. Who could even have killed Jenna himself. Another part of me wished that Jenna was somewhere far away from here, living her life to the full. Maybe she really had run away and started a new life. Maybe she was happy. Had children. A husband. A career. But as soon as the thought flitted into my head, it was gone again. Deep in my heart I knew that wasn't true. And a while later so did everyone else.

CHAPTER TWENTY-ONE

———

The tavern had been empty—probably due to the crime scene vans blatantly advertising something going on out there, putting people off from coming in—so luckily there were no customers inside when Lester made his announcement.

He sat at the bar, Harvey seated next to him. "We've found the remains of a skeleton. The medical examiner has confirmed as best as she can at this stage that the bones are consistent with a body being placed in there sometime in the last twenty-five years. She's contacted a forensic anthropologist who will be arriving soon to consult with us and make a more accurate analysis. But under the circumstances, we believe this is Jenna Williams."

I blew out a breath. Poor Jenna.

"Do you know how she died?" Vernon asked.

"It looks like she was strangled," Lester said. "She was found with a belt still wrapped around her neck—although the material had decayed a bit, the buckle is still intact. It's quite distinctive—a metal Celtic cross design. I'm guessing there was some kind of argument between Tim and Jenna, and he lost his temper and killed her before dumping her body there."

My hand flew to my cheek. The ground outside on the cliffs was naturally uneven, so I wasn't surprised someone had managed to hide her body out there without it being discovered.

"Which just goes to prove my theory," Lester said smugly. "Tim killed Jenna and then killed Pandora to keep her quiet. I'm going to get a double homicide out of this one." Lester rubbed his hands together and stood. "Well, I can't sit around here chatting all day. I've got more work to do." He strutted outside.

"I need a drink," Harvey said, his tanned face turned pale.

"Me too," I said.

Vernon poured us all a shot of Jack Daniel's on the rocks.

Harvey gulped his greedily. I sipped mine, trying to take it all in, not knowing what to think. Vernon was just about to take a sip of his drink when Ruby waltzed in.

"What's going on?" She pointed outside. "Lester Marshall and some crime scene people are out there at Harvey's dig site."

"Didn't you get my text?" I asked.

"No, I haven't checked my phone." She eyed Vernon's drink. "Are you drinking again? You know what the doctor said! No more alcohol! Honestly, what's the point of making all these healing foods for you, when you carry on with your old ways?"

"Murder trumps abstinence any day," Vernon said, sitting down at a barstool before giving her an update. He shook his now half-empty glass at her. "Want one now?"

She took his and downed it in one. "This is just...incredible."

"Strangling is a crime of passion," Vernon said.

"So was I right about Tim, then? Did he kill Jenna, then murder Pandora after all, to keep her quiet?" Ruby asked.

"Lester Marshall still thinks so," Vernon said, although he didn't sound convinced.

CHAPTER TWENTY-TWO

———

I kept the tavern closed for the three days it took the police and crime scene techs to sift through the area. Because of Harvey and Carmen's work recovering the ancient relics and bones near to where the new skeleton had been discovered, they were on hand to advise officials exactly what they'd been doing there.

The only good news to come out of it all was that it meant when they packed up their equipment and left, Harvey had some free time while the forensic team examined the bones and surrounding soil samples more thoroughly. And I decided that I might as well keep the place closed for one more day out of respect for Jenna's memory, so Harvey and I were finally able to spend some quality time together.

He knocked on the outer door to my apartment at 10:00 a.m., picnic basket in hand, and a warm but worried smile on his face. "I need a break from all this business with Jenna's remains." He stared intensely into my eyes. "We've both been so distracted and busy. It would be nice to switch off from everything." He set the basket down on the step and pulled me into his arms. "I thought we could get away from it all for the day."

I nestled against his shoulder, kissing his neck. Mmmm, that was so good.

"Or maybe not," he whispered huskily into my ear, his warm breath igniting a fire inside. "We could just stay here all day. Have a picnic in bed?"

I didn't need to be asked twice. I wanted him. Wanted him to fill my mind and body and replace the horrible thoughts about Jenna and Pandora and Carmen roaming around.

I gave him a hungry smile and tugged on his hand, leading him up the stairs, where we were suddenly lost in a tangle of clothes and sheets and kisses, and the stresses of the past few months drifted to the far edge of my brain.

It was magical, sensual, healing. Just what I needed.

Afterward, I lay in the crook of his arm as he traced his fingertip around in a pattern on my shoulder. I wanted to ask him about Carmen. About what she'd meant to him. Whether she *still* meant anything, but I couldn't bring myself to in case I didn't like the answer. I wanted to concentrate on the moment and appreciate the right now before it slipped away and became another memory.

"Are you hungry?" he asked later.

I grinned. "Starved."

We devoured our feast in the bed. This was exactly what I needed. Lost in our own little cocoon world, talking, laughing.

"So, what do you fancy doing now?" Harvey asked. "We've still got the whole afternoon ahead of us."

"You know what I'd really like to do? But I don't know if you'll want to."

He cocked an eyebrow. "I thought we just did. And I *definitely* wanted to."

I laughed, nudging him with my arm. "I want to go diving again." I'd dived a lot when I was traveling the world, and I loved the magical, mystical quality of the ocean. Being underwater, the only sound in your ears from your own breathing, the sense of being away from everything, all the worries and stress, lost in a vast marine world under the surface. I'd only dived once since being in Danger Cove, and that was also with Harvey when I was trying to help him out by searching for the *Ocean's Revenge*. "But you've been diving all the time looking for the ship, so maybe you want to do something else on your day off?"

He shrugged. "Well, I never say no to diving, so let's do it! My equipment is in a locker at the diving center in the harbor, and you can hire some there again. Where do you want to go?"

"How about we kill two birds with one stone? We can cover an area you've marked out on your search grid for the *Ocean's Revenge*."

"A busman's holiday, then?"

"A what?"

"It means a holiday or recreational activity that involves doing the same thing as your job."

"Oh, right!"

"Sounds like a plan to me." He grinned.

An hour later, we were leaving the harbor on the *Meant to Be*, a boat owned by the University of Washington that Harvey was using while he was in town. I thought about the first kiss we'd shared, right on this very boat two months ago. Were we meant to be? Or were Harvey and Carmen? I mentally flushed the idea of them together out to sea.

We headed left past the lighthouse, where Jenna had apparently gone to meet Tim the night she'd disappeared. It wasn't far from there to the cliffs in front of the Smugglers' Tavern, but still no witnesses had seen her. I pictured her arguing with Tim, trying to break up with him. He was angry. Not wanting her to leave him. Not wanting her to go to Seattle to start her new job. If he couldn't have her, then why should someone else? In my head, I saw him remove his belt, loop it round her neck, and squeeze with all his strength until her eyes rolled back and she collapsed. Then an image of Ian came into my head, strangling her because he was jealous of his sister. Poor Jenna. I forced the image away. Today was about having fun and forgetting all the bad things that had happened lately.

Harvey released the anchor when we got to a spot parallel to the cliffs below the tavern. We donned our equipment, checked it before checking each other's, then he handed me a mesh bag to clip to my dive belt, in case we came across any other artifacts from the ship.

"I found the hull section right out there." He pointed to the water. "Fingers crossed we can find some more today. You ready?"

"Absolutely." I gave him a thumbs-up.

We climbed down the ladder into the sea. It was calm today, perfect diving conditions. We swam through the deep blue down to the ocean floor, flippers moving in time with each other. Everything seemed to take on a slow-motion quality down here, as if time were suspended. It was liberating, exhilarating.

I scanned the sandy bottom, spotting a dogfish and a giant pacific octopus, the reddish-brown tentacles slithering across a pile of empty shells near the entrance to a small hole in some rocks. Someone had eaten dinner. I spotted a piece of metal buried in the sand. As I retrieved it, I noticed it was a tarnished goblet. The kind that may have been used to drink wine in olden days. Unsure if it had come from the *Ocean's Revenge*, or been lost at sea some other way, I placed it in my bag anyway for Harvey to check out later. Ten minutes into the dive, I spotted a dorsal fin about fifteen meters directly ahead of me.

I wasn't too worried about sharks. I'd studied the great whites for a volunteer project in Australia and dived with reef sharks, lemon sharks, and hammerheads before. As far as I was concerned, they had a bad rap. But my heart rate did kick up a notch for a moment, before realizing this was actually a Pacific white-sided dolphin.

I tugged Harvey's arm. He was so intent on brushing the sand away from the bottom, examining a piece of wood, that he hadn't noticed the dolphin. Pointing to the beautiful cetacean, I noticed more of them rummaging around in the sand with their rostrums, or noses, and playing with each other or pieces of flotsam. One had a ring of seaweed on its flipper and darted through the water before it fell off and another picked it up by the rostrum. I'd never seen them this close up before, only from a boat, and this was too magical an event to pass by.

We swam nearer toward them, hoping they'd stick around. I knew they could travel around forty miles an hour, so if they didn't want us there, we'd have no chance of keeping up. But they were content to play around us, gliding through the water effortlessly, and it almost seemed as if they were waiting for us to catch up. As we got within a couple of meters, I noticed some babies swimming underneath their mothers.

The whole pod consisted of around twenty-five dolphins, some with scars on their skin from boats or fights. They let us swim along with them, side by side, as they surfaced to breathe, then sunk down again in unison. One pair of dolphins was mating right in front of us! I stared in wonder at the magical sight, something I'd only ever seen before on the National Geographic channel.

Four dolphins broke away from the pod, treating us to an underwater acrobatic show as they looped around each other in an elegant dance. As we sliced through the water, one dolphin came right alongside me, so close I could look into its eye. It seemed to be sending me a message: *Yes, I know you're there, and I'm letting you swim with me!* Goose bumps broke out over my skin that had nothing to do with the water temperature. It was a spiritual, special moment, because when I looked into its eye, I could see the intelligence behind it. Could feel the sentient spirit of this incredible creature.

Bubbles of air rose from their blowholes, and I heard them communicating with each other through clicks and whistles. We swam with them for another five minutes, and I noticed a dolphin at the rear of the pod, lagging behind. It had a tangle of fishing line that wrapped around one pectoral fin and its body, restricting the movement in the fin and cutting into its flesh.

I tugged Harvey's arm and pointed out the dolphin, then pointed to the knife strapped in a holster around his leg. He nodded, and we swam toward it.

When we were both along the side of its injured fin, the dolphin slowed almost to a stop in a vertical position, rostrum facing the sky, its fluke pointing down to the ocean floor. I sent it silent messages. *Hold on, baby. We're trying to help you.* It looked into my eyes, and again I was hit with that same sense of intelligence and understanding. It stayed where it was, perfectly calm, almost still, as I took hold of the wire, trying to ease it a little way from the surface of its skin so Harvey could slice through it without cutting the animal.

Won't be long, baby. You're doing great!

Harvey worked quickly, cutting, while I removed parts of the wire.

Just one more bit, and we're done!

He unwound the final piece of wire from around its body, and the dolphin flapped its pectoral fin at us. Then it lifted its fluke, maneuvering into a horizontal position directly in front of us. We were nose to nose, with only about a foot between us. It shook its head left to right, up and down, then swam around us in a circle, flapping the now free fin in a move that I knew was its own special way of saying thank you.

Slowly, the dolphin headed toward the rest of the pod, letting us swim alongside it as it rejoined the group.

We stayed with them for a while longer, and as much as I hated to leave them, I knew our oxygen tanks would be getting low. I checked my equipment and signaled Harvey that I needed to go up. Taking one last look at the dolphins, and sending them all a silent thank-you of my own for letting me into their underwater world, I kicked my way to the surface. Treading water, I lifted my mask to my forehead.

When Harvey appeared, I said, "Oh. Wow! How amazing was that?" My whole body was tingling with the excitement of it all.

He removed his snorkel, his wide, elated smile matching mine. "Bloody hell, that was fantastic! I'm so glad we managed to get that wire off. I was worried I was going to cut into the skin, but...oh my God. Just..." He shook his head, suddenly speechless.

"It was awesome!" I shouted up to the sky. "Swim safe, dolphins!"

He pulled me closer. "I'm so glad I got to witness such a special moment with such a special person."

* * *

An hour later, we were back on dry land, chattering constantly about the mind-blowing experience we'd just had, with huge grins that hadn't left our faces. On a high, we drove back to my apartment above the tavern, then Harvey took a shower while I made a platter of meze from items I had in the fridge: olives, feta cheese, smoked salmon, sliced organic tomatoes, hummus, roasted vegetable chips, and some thyme and garlic chickpea flour bread I'd bought from Veggie Tables. When he was finished, I jumped into the shower too, still marveling at the amazing day we'd had together.

I was just getting dressed, when someone knocked on the outer door, and I heard voices. I wrapped a towel around my wet hair and walked into the lounge. Ruby and Vernon were in there. Harvey was picking at the meze in the kitchen, leaning over the open-plan counter and telling them about our awesome experience.

"Hey, sweetie." Ruby kissed me on both cheeks. "Sounds like you had a fantastic day."

"It was spectacular! Are you guys hungry? I made some nibbles. There's plenty of it."

"I'm hungry. I'm not exactly getting full up on smashed avocado club on gluten-free bread and pasta with rocket and pine nut pesto," Vernon complained. "I need some meat. Fries would be good too, followed by chili and a huge burger. No, make that a triple burger. And a chocolate fudge sundae. Or maybe a hot brownie slathered with melting ice cream."

Ruby flashed him a withering look and helped me bring the platter and plates over.

"We've got some news." Vernon sat at the small dining room table that had previously been in my rental cottage. It looked out of place here in the large room. I'd toyed with the idea of buying new stuff for the apartment. It wasn't like I couldn't afford it now. But I wasn't used to having such wealth and being able to have luxuries, and it felt odd to squander things away when the table was still in perfectly good working order.

I made tea for Ruby and I, and coffee for Harvey and Vernon, as they chatted about the awful discovery on my land.

"So, what have you found out?" I asked Vernon, sitting down and popping an olive in my mouth.

Vernon broke a piece of toasted chickpea bread apart and stared at it. "This isn't real bread."

"It's gluten free," I said. "From Veggie Tables."

He sniffed it. Shrugged. Dunked it in some hummus and took a bite.

"It's lovely," Ruby said.

"Tastes like sawdust." Vernon pulled off a bigger chunk and stuffed that in his mouth.

"Yeah?" Ruby said. "Well, if it tastes so bad, why are you eating so much of it?"

"I'm hungry! Anyway, wait till you hear this." He looked at me. "Donna's confessed to killing Jenna."

My eyes nearly popped out. "What? After all this time?"

"It's just a terrible shame she didn't do it before Pandora died." Ruby traced her fingertip around the edge of her cup.

"Blimey." Harvey ran a hand through his hair.

Vernon leaned his elbows on the table. "Apparently, when Donna met Tim at the university, she wanted to be more than friends. She was in love with him, obsessively so, but he was seeing Jenna at the time. My contact told me Donna said she knew if she could get rid of Jenna that she and Tim could be together."

I shook my head, flabbergasted.

"On the night of the fair, Donna saw Tim there and asked if he wanted to watch the fireworks with her later on, but he said he couldn't, as he'd arranged to meet Jenna at the lighthouse. Donna figured that was her perfect opportunity, so she found Jenna and told her Tim had asked her to pass on a message that the meeting spot had been changed to the tavern. The place was closed that night because of the festivities in town. Donna followed Jenna up there, then strangled her with her belt."

I thought about Jenna, who was petite and fragile looking, and Donna, who was tall and big boned. And with an insane jealousy spurring her on, I supposed it would have been easy to overpower Jenna, especially if she was taken by surprise. "How did she hide the body?"

"She found some garden tools in the storage barn at the back of the tavern, dug a hole, dragged Jenna down there, and buried her."

"Didn't anyone notice the area had been disturbed when they were all out searching for Jenna?" Harvey asked.

"Donna said she took a lot of time covering the exposed soil with rocks and patches of grass from other areas of the cliffs outside the tavern so it wasn't obvious. And we all know how uneven and rocky that land is."

"But what about Pandora?" I asked. "I thought Donna was in the shop at the time Pandora was murdered, so who killed her?"

"Lester now thinks that when Pandora called Tim that day, she'd worked out somehow that Donna had killed Jenna and wanted to tell Tim about it. But Tim wanted it covered up so

Donna wouldn't go to prison, and became so angry he killed Pandora to shut her up." Vernon shook his head. "Lester thinks they were both protecting each other to stop the truth from coming out."

"Like some kind of Bonnie and Clyde!" Ruby gasped.

I sat back, stunned, letting it sink in. Something was still bugging me, but I couldn't work out what.

"Unless Donna is actually covering for Tim," Ruby suggested. "If she knew all along Tim had killed Jenna, maybe she's confessed in order to cast reasonable doubt to try to get him off for Pandora's murder?" Ruby suggested.

"No, I think this throws a totally different light on things. When Donna heard about her belt being found with Jenna, she knew the game was up. It would probably only have been a matter of time before someone who knew her back then identified it." Vernon stared out of the window into the dusky sunset. "Looks like we were wrong about Tim's guilt all along, and Lester's theory is right, even though I hate to admit it. Donna killed Jenna out of jealousy. Then Tim killed Pandora to protect Donna and stop everyone from learning the truth"

"It's so sad," Ruby said. "Donna obviously didn't know Jenna was meeting Tim that night to break off their relationship. If she had, things could've turned out so differently for everyone." Ruby slipped a slice of tomato into her mouth. "I spoke to Ian this morning. The police told him about the latest development."

"How did he take it?" Harvey asked.

She chewed and swallowed. "I think he was still in shock, not surprisingly. The police called him this morning to let him know they'd matched Jenna's dental records to the skeleton they found here. So at least he's finally got some answers. He wanted to postpone Pandora's funeral until they release Jenna's remains. He wants Jenna and Pandora to be buried next to each other in a single ceremony. He thinks it's what they both would've wanted."

"I'll let Tara know." I stood up and grabbed my cell from my bag, dialing her number. Since Tara was doing the catering for the wake, we'd have to try to salvage what food we'd already bought for it. Luckily, Tara came up with the bright idea of turning the surplus food into a couple of specials on the menu, so it would all be recycled to good use. "So, that's it, then." I shook the niggling feeling away and sat back in the chair, lacing my fingers through Harvey's. "The killers are in custody, and Ian can hopefully start to move on with his life."

CHAPTER TWENTY-THREE

———

We had a busload of tourists in the tavern the next day, along with a whole bunch of locals wanting to find out what the gossip was about Jenna and Pandora. I tried to answer their questions politely without giving too much away, and I was glad it was busy so I didn't have time to stop and chat to people. The day passed in a blur of potato wedges, cocktails, and daily specials.

Carmen sashayed in about 7:00 p.m., dressed in tight leggings and a low-cut top, and sat at a booth, tapping her fingernails on the table as she studied the menu.

I walked over to her table, pad and pen poised. "Hi, can I get you something?" *A new personality, maybe?*

She put the menu down and gave me a snooty look. "Actually, I wanted to talk to you. About Harvey."

Uh-oh! I could guess what was coming. Harvey had decided he'd rather be with Carmen than me. They'd rekindled their relationship, and yesterday was just his way of saying good-bye. Is that what Harvey had been trying to tell me all along when we kept getting interrupted?

I sat opposite her, wanting to hear what she had to say and not wanting to at the same time.

"You know I told you Harvey and I used to be together?"

"Yes." I swallowed back the bitter taste in my mouth.

"Our relationship lasted a year." She leaned forward, eyes formed into thin slits. "One year! And we were good together. We met at work and fell in love. Then suddenly he started becoming obsessed with the *Ocean's Revenge* and persuaded our boss to let him come out to this"—she glanced around the room as if searching for a suitable word—"this crap hole and look for it. He only came here to put a notch on his career, you know. And when we've finished this recovery, we'll both be going back to the UK. *Together*! So you might as well stop things with him now. You're only going to get hurt when he comes back to me."

Anger was bubbling to the surface now. How dare she! I took a deep breath, trying to think of something polite to say, but I was struggling. *Do not lower yourself to her level!* "And what does Harvey think about that?" I folded my arms and waited for her answer.

"Harvey wants to get back with me, but he's too shy to tell you himself. I just need *you* to get the message, too, and leave him alone." She poked a finger in my direction. "Leave *us* alone so we can get on with our lives without your interference."

"Actually, that's not what Harvey thinks at all." Harvey's voice sounded to our right. I'd been so busy concentrating on not swearing at Carmen or poking her eyes out with the toothpicks on the table that I hadn't noticed his approach. Neither had Carmen.

Carmen stood up, a saccharine-sweet smile on her face. "Of course it is, babe. You only ended things with me because you were coming here. You still love me. You know you do." She ran a hand up and down his arm.

Harvey glanced around the busy tavern. Luckily, the hum of talking, scraping of cutlery on plates, and the music were drowning out what we were saying. He sighed and gave Carmen a sympathetic frown. Then sat next to me. "Look, Carmen, we went through this before I left England. You know things weren't working out between us. It was time to move on. For both of us. I'm sorry if you still believe otherwise, but it's over."

"So why did you ask me to come out here and help you then?" she screeched. "You wanted me back but were too shy to say it to my face!"

"I didn't ask for you! It was Steve's decision who to send out here to assist me. He told me he was going to send Kevin! I didn't know until you got here that he'd changed his mind."

She folded her arms, hugging her elbows, her gaze darting between Harvey and me, finally taking in what Harvey had said. "Well, how cozy for you both," she snapped viciously.

"I'm sorry, Carmen, but it's finished between us. It has been for a long time," Harvey carried on. He grabbed hold of my hand and squeezed it. "I'm with Hope now."

Carmen leaped to her feet, lips in a puckered scowl, fists balled at her hips. "Well, not for long! You're making a big mistake!" She treated me to a final glare before flouncing out.

"What do you think she meant by that?" I looked at Harvey.

"I'm not sure. She can be a bit unpredictable and highly strung at times." He twisted in his seat to face me, his arm sliding over the backrest toward my shoulders. "I've been trying to tell you about what happened with her, but we either keep getting interrupted or it never seems like the right time."

I held a hand up to stop him. "You don't have to tell me. We all have a past. All have previous relationships. I knew she was your ex and guessed she was still in love with you, but I just needed to know that you didn't feel the same."

"I don't. It was over long before I came out here, despite what she said. I don't know why it took me a whole year to work out that she wasn't a genuine person. It's been difficult though. We obviously still have to work together, so I was trying to be as gentle as possible about the split. Looks like she wouldn't take no for an answer though." He pulled me toward him, his lips close to my ear, breath tickling my skin, sending goose bumps darting all over. "What I've been trying to tell you is…there's no one else but you, Hope. How could there be when I'm stupidly in love with you?"

My heart did a little happy sigh.

I wrapped my hand around his neck and kissed him, but before I could tell him the same, his phone rang out.

"I guess you'd better get that. It could be important," I said. "I'm not going anywhere."

Harvey groaned and pulled his phone from his pocket, looking at the screen. "It's Lester Marshall." He answered and had a quick conversation that involved a lot of "yes" and "okay" answers. He hung up and turned to me. "Sorry, they want me back at the forensic lab in Seattle to finalize something to do with Jenna's remains. I have to sign a statement about my involvement with the site."

"Okay, go." I gave him a gentle push. "What I have to say can wait."

He kissed me, and I watched him walk out the door.

He loves me.

I couldn't wipe the happy smile off my face for the rest of the night.

"Someone's had some good news." Ruby cocked her head with a grin later as the crowds began to peter out. "What was all that about with Carmen and Harvey?"

I filled her in on the details.

"See, I told you everything would work out okay." She tapped her nose knowingly. "Maybe I should buy a hat for the wedding. We could do with some happy news around here."

I held my hand up and laughed. "Whoa! Now you're getting way ahead of yourself."

"Stop hassling the poor girl," Vernon said.

"I'm not hassling her. I'm projecting."

"Projecting? What are you raving on about?"

"If you want something, you have to project your intentions out to the Universe and visualize it happening. That's how you manifest your desires."

"Really?" Vernon closed his eyes, arms moving in exaggerated circular motions as if he was doing some kind of conjuring trick. "Oh, yes, I can see it now." He snapped his fingers. "I'm projecting a thick, juicy steak with all the trimmings. I can visualize it. A dash of mustard. Chunky fries. Onion rings. A side of slaw and—"

"Oh, stop it!" Ruby elbowed him gently.

His eyelids shot open, giving her an innocent, "*What?*"

After closing time, I kissed them both good-bye and locked up the tavern's front door. Flicking off the lights, I made my way along the internal corridor and up the stairs to my apartment.

Zen was waiting behind the door, staring at me expectantly.

I picked him up. "And what mischief have you been up to since I've been gone?" I plonked him down in the kitchen and refilled his and Karma's bowls. I glanced around for Karma, who usually came at the slightest sound of chow. "Where's Karma?" I asked Zen.

He glanced around briefly before tucking in.

I called out to my kitten and searched the apartment, but he was nowhere to be seen. Maybe he'd gone out the kitty door and not been able to get back inside for some reason. I headed down the other staircase that led to the external door and unlocked it, stepping into the darkness and being treated to a blast of cold night air. The only light came from the full moon glowing above my head and the abundance of stars shimmering in the coal-black sky.

"Karma! Chow time!" I called out. No sign of him. Usually, he didn't stray far—he was much too timid, and he hated being without Zen, so I was starting to worry now. "Karma!" I walked around the outside of the tavern.

Wait, what's that? I thought I heard a sound in between the waves crashing against the rocks below the tavern. Was it some kind of muffled mewing? "Karma?"

I strained my ears, listening. Another sound then. Like a groan. And it was coming from...where? My head spun around, trying to locate the source of the noise. "Hello? Is someone out here?"

"Get me out of here, you idiot! I think I've broken my leg!" It was Carmen's voice, mixed with a definite meowing sound, and it came from the entrance to the caves behind the tent.

I rushed over, stumbling on a patch of uneven ground. Pulling the flap back, I peered inside the tent, but it was so dark I couldn't see much. I pulled my cell from my pocket and turned on the flashlight app, pointing it down into the dark entrance to the caves.

Carmen lay sprawled on her back, one leg bent at an unnatural angle. Karma was trying to scramble up the ladder at the entrance.

"Omigod! What happened? Are you okay? Is Karma okay?"

Carmen glared at me, then winced and groaned. The light from my phone reflected off her pale face. "Sod the cat! Get me out! I'm in"—she took a deep breath—"agony!"

I dialed the emergency services, asking for an ambulance and a fire truck, then climbed down the ladder. Karma leaped up at me, begging to be in my arms. I picked him up, cradling him as he nestled into my elbow. "What happened, Carmen? Can you move?" I crouched down in front of her on the rocky ground. "The ambulance is on its way. They'll be here in no time. Don't worry. What were you doing out here in the dark?"

"It was that stupid cat! I tripped over it and fell..." She groaned again, reaching out to touch her leg, then thinking better of it and resting her head back on a rock. Tears of pain sprang into her eyes. Beads of sweat broke out on her upper lip.

I glanced down at Karma, who'd buried his head into my skin, trembling. "But Karma's scared of this tent. He never comes near here, so how could you trip over him and fall in?" Then I noticed some fresh scratches on her arms. Scratches that looked suspiciously like claw marks. And that wasn't all. There was a dead fish lying next to her foot. "Did you do something to my cat?"

"Don't be stupid."

"Well, what's this fish doing here? Were you trying to entice Karma into this hole? You've got scratch marks on your arms."

"I was trying to teach *you* a lesson to stay away from my man!"

"By doing what?" I held Karma tighter, stroking his shivering body.

"You stole something I love from me, so I was going to do the same to you!" she spat.

"What, by leaving a poor defenseless kitten down here to starve?" I asked incredulously. "Is that what you were up to?"

"Yes, that's exactly what I was going to do. It's only a cat!"

"How low can you get!" I fought the urge to kick her broken leg really hard, instead feeling all over Karma's tiny soft body, checking for broken bones.

"Oh, shut up," she snarled. "If I hadn't tripped over the stupid thing when he leapt out of my arms, you'd never have known it was me."

When the sirens and flashing lights appeared in the parking lot, I climbed out of the cave, clutching my terrified cat toward me. Part of me felt bad that I'd previously wished Carmen to fall down the hole and break her leg. But because of what she'd been about to do, the other part of me thought it was Karma. Literally.

CHAPTER TWENTY-FOUR

It took ten minutes for the fire service to hoist Carmen out of the cave and load her onto a gurney. After what she'd done, I didn't really want to go with her to the hospital, but who else could I call to make sure she was okay? Harvey was tied up with the police, and she didn't really know anyone else in town. And I was hoping to win back some good brownie points after all the lying I'd done recently trying to solve Pandora's murder.

While Carmen was being moved into the back of the ambulance, I took a traumatized Karma back to the house. As soon as he saw Zen, he rushed toward him, and Zen gave him some reassuring licks. I locked the kitty door so neither of them could get back out, then hotfooted it back to the ambulance in time to hear Carmen screaming at them to give her some pain meds. "Morphine! I want morphine, you idiots!"

I climbed in and sat on a foldaway seat by the door, watching the paramedic open a plastic syringe packet, discarding the wrapper hurriedly on the floor. He filled it from a vial of some kind of liquid and gave her a shot. After that, Carmen was quiet, eyes closed as we sped to the Seattle General Hospital.

She was wheeled down a corridor, and I was directed to a packed waiting room. I picked up a magazine, flicking through but unable to register anything. I was seething at her, but I did some deep breathing to try to keep calm, and opened and closed my jaw to get rid of the knot of muscles tightening up. How could any sane person want to harm a defenseless animal like that just to get back at someone? I fantasized about doing some martial arts moves on her but couldn't decide what I wanted to do first. A flying knee? An uppercut elbow? Oooh, a double chop elbow would be good.

I slammed the magazine down on top of a pile on a table and tried to project something positive into my head to dispel the angry energy, like Harvey telling me he loved me. Ruby had suggested to me that inner anger was a destructive emotion. The person you were angry with probably didn't know or didn't even care if you felt like that, so why store it up? The only person anger hurt was you, which was why I meditated a lot and tried to practice the art of forgiveness. Okay, so obviously I sometimes needed a bit of help to maintain that, but at least I was trying.

I attempted to clear my mind of Carmen, but instead, I kept seeing her in the ambulance, screaming for pain meds, and the paramedic's syringe wrapper on the floor, hastily discarded. There was something about it that triggered an idea, but it was just out of reach. What was it?

Before I could think anymore, I saw Ian striding down the ER corridor, dressed in a white doctor's coat, heading toward the front doors.

He spotted me and walked over. "Hi. I didn't expect to see you here. Are you okay?"

"Oh, I'm fine. I just came with..." I searched for the right word to call Carmen. A psycho? A jealous freak? *No, be kind, Hope.* "I came with someone who needed treatment. I'm just waiting to make sure they're okay."

"Well, you can't have cycled all the way here. Do you need a ride back to Danger Cove? I'd be happy to give you a lift. After everything you've done for me lately, it would be my pleasure."

"Um...I need to check on Carmen first. Find out if she needs any help getting back."

He nodded. "I can get an update on your friend and find out what's happening." He disappeared behind the triage desk, chatting with one of the nurses. Then he walked back up the corridor.

A few minutes later, he returned. "She's still waiting for her leg to be set in a cast. Then they're going to keep her in overnight, just for observation. It seems she also hit her head, so they want to monitor her for any concussion."

Hopefully the bang to her noggin finally knocked some sense into her.

"Oh, okay," I said, tucking a wayward wave behind my ear. "In that case, I'd love a ride back, thanks."

I followed him out to his Range Rover in the car park and buckled up. "So how're you doing?"

"I don't know. My head's still a mess, but at least Tim's been arrested for both Jenna's and Mother's murders now." He paused before starting the ignition and driving off. "You know, I never really got say good-bye to either of them. When Jenna went to meet Tim that day, I was out with my friends. I can't even remember what I was doing now. And when I left town after everything went wrong between Mother and me, I didn't have the courage to tell her I was going. I waited till she was asleep and left a note. By that time it wasn't like we had much of a relationship. We never really did. It was always mother and Jenna. Deep down, I don't think she ever wanted me. Of course, things were okay when Father was alive. But when he died...well, I was the odd one out."

I reached out and put my hand on his arm. "I'm sorry. I know it's difficult when relationships go wrong. Just because people are your family doesn't mean you're always bound by unconditional love. Some things just aren't meant to be. But I bet it's made you a stronger person. The person you are today. Everything is a lesson, designed to make us learn something valuable. Sometimes you don't know what that lesson is until later in life, but it's necessary nevertheless. And you can't change the past. It's not healthy to let it eat you up. You can say good-bye now, to both of them. Then you can let it go. All the guilt and the anger and the feelings of inadequacy and hurt."

He picked up a water bottle from the drink holder in the center console, and I let my hand fall away. He took a long swig and swallowed. "Sounds like you've been through something similar."

I shrugged. "Yeah, my parents...well, let's just say they weren't there for me either. I pretty much raised myself. And like you, as soon as I was old enough, I left. But what I learned eventually was to not have any regrets about the way things turned out. Regrets waste too much negative time and energy. And happiness is an inside job. You can spend all your time searching for something, wanting things to have been different, thinking if you do this or that, or get this or that, it will make you happy, but it won't. You have to take control of yourself, and that starts with self-love." I fiddled with my tiger's-eye bracelet, wondering how I'd ever let Carmen make me doubt myself and raise old anxieties and fears that I wasn't good enough to the surface. I wasn't in competition with anyone. I was just me. And I was happy with who I was. Carmen, on the other hand, was superficial and nasty. She may have been beautiful on the outside, but inside she was total ugliness. Why would I want to be like her?

"You know, I think you're right." He raised his bottle to me in a *cheers* gesture. Took another sip. "The day before Mother died, I was coming to see her. I'd spent too much time searching for…I don't know…*something*. Something missing in my life. I thought *things* could make me happy. Make me feel worthy. Material things. So I worked hard, built up my practice, bought stuff. Enjoyed the fancy holidays and the fast cars and splashed money around like it was going out of fashion. Because it got the girls, you know. Until I realized they weren't with me because of me. They were only hanging around because they thought I was rich. And then things started to go wrong at work. I lost interest in it all. Couldn't even see why I'd become a doctor in the first place. Started to question everything. Turned to gambling and became addicted to that. Overran my credit and started building up debts that I couldn't control. Maybe I was having a midlife crisis. I don't know. And then I decided I needed help, so I checked myself into an inpatient gambling addiction program a few weeks ago. I had a lot of time in there in between group and one-to-one therapy to think, and I started dealing with the past. Mother, Father, Jenna. We all suffered tragedies, but mother and I were the only ones left. I realized I had to try to finally patch things up between us before it was too late."

"So what happened?"

"I got out of the program on Labor Day, and the next morning I drove to Danger Cove. I parked outside Mother's house. Walked up the path and stood on her doorstep. I was about to knock, but then I thought about everything that had happened. About all the time that had gone by. And…I lost my nerve. I couldn't do it. I was scared. Still not ready to confront everything that had happened in the past. I didn't want to be rejected by her again like I'd felt all those years growing up. So I got into my car and drove back to Seattle. I was so mixed up and emotional that I ran into a stop sign on the way out of town."

"I heard about that."

"I got a phone call from an Officer Faria a few days later, who said there were some witnesses. I could either pay for it to be repaired or be charged with damaging it. He's the same guy who caught me speeding the day mother was killed."

"Yeah, about that...so you came back a second time to see Pandora?"

He nodded. "I drove around town for a while, trying to work up the courage, but again, I just couldn't bring myself to speak to her. There was still too much pent-up anger and hurt. I wanted to get it out, but at the same time, I didn't. Does that sound crazy?"

My heart ached for him. "No. It doesn't sound crazy at all. It sounds pretty normal under the circumstances."

Ian sank into a silence. I opened my mouth to say more but didn't really know what to say. Ian had to grieve in his own way. Get past his own guilt about the past and hopefully move forward and make peace with himself. I looked out of the window and watched the world speed by.

Finally, we pulled up in the tavern's parking lot. He got out and walked to the passenger side, opening the door for me. "Will you be coming to the funeral? Jenna's remains have been released now, so I can arrange for a double service. I've changed my mind about having the wake here. I hope you don't mind. But what with Jenna being found out there..." He trailed off, eyes glistening. He cleared his throat and coughed.

"Of course I don't mind. But I'm happy to do anything I can to help." I gave him a hug. "Just let me know the date, okay?"

"I'll see you soon, then."

I stood and watched him walk back around the car, his shoulders hunched, head down, then I took a deep breath and headed inside.

Karma didn't seem to have any long-lasting effects from his earlier brush with Carmen and, along with Zen, was ecstatic to see me when I opened the door, winding himself around my legs and purring loudly before I could even get up the stairs. I refilled their bowls of food and poured myself a much-needed glass of red wine, staring out the window at the full moon illuminating the water, watching the swell and fall of the waves crashing onto the rocks below the lighthouse as everything turned over in my head.

I thought about Pandora's murder. How the killer had left the same kind of wrapper on the floor as the paramedic had in the ambulance. How the syringe was still left in Pandora's vein when we'd found her. The vial of pentobarbital on her kitchen table.

And I wondered again why the killer didn't take the evidence with him when he left the house.

Donna's words filtered into my head: *It was probably some kind of trap.*

I knew then what it was that had been bugging me about it all. Pandora had called Tim at 12:02 p.m., asking him to visit her at 3:30 p.m., but she knew by then that she already had a prearranged appointment with Ruby and me at 4:00 p.m. She must've known the conversation would get heated. That it would turn into an argument. Pandora still adamantly believed Tim had killed Jenna. Her intention was to plead with Tim to get a confession out of him so she could finally lay her daughter to rest before she died from the inoperable brain tumor. But Pandora wouldn't have known how long it would take to get such a confession, if at all, so why did she only allow half an hour's meeting before we turned up? Surely she would've kept the whole afternoon free.

And that's when it hit me. Pandora's death really was tied to Jenna's, just not in the way I'd thought.

CHAPTER TWENTY-FIVE

———

Pandora knew she was dying. And she was sure Tim had killed Jenna. She wasn't trying to get a confession from Tim at all that day, because she didn't think he'd ever admit it after all these years. What she'd intended all along was to frame him for her murder. If she couldn't get him convicted of Jenna's death, she'd choose the next best thing. She'd *planned* it so we would arrive in time to see Tim leaving. A lot of people in town thought Tim had got away with murder and had a huge motive to kill Pandora. He had access to the pentobarbital. And if he was seen leaving the house around the time of her death, it would seem like an open-and-shut case. And it did to Lester Marshall.

That's why the wrapper was still on the floor, discarded in a hurry. She couldn't remove the needle from her arm because the drug had worked so quickly she was dead before she'd even finished shooting the whole amount into her vein.

Pandora had taken her own life. And Tim really had been framed.

I sat in the interview room at the police station with Vernon, going over my theory with Lester. When I'd finished, I said, "That's why the only prints you found on the syringe and vial were Pandora's."

He stared at me incredulously. Then he snorted. "That's the craziest thing I've ever heard."

"It's not crazy when you think about it. It all fits into place," Vernon said.

Lester narrowed his eyes. It looked like he was thinking it over, but you could never tell with him. He could equally have been thinking about which flavor pizza he was going to order for lunch.

"Pandora was dying anyway and knew this was her last chance, her only chance, to get her revenge on Tim. She trained as a nurse years ago, so she knew how to inject herself with the pentobarbital," I said.

"What about the cell phone she used to call Tim? How do you explain that? If she was going to kill herself and wasn't worried about him suing her or getting her arrested for harassment, why throw it over her fence after she made the call?"

"I don't know," I said.

"Maybe to create more confusion and suspicion and point it toward Tim calling her," Vernon suggested. "She must've been under a terrible amount of stress at the end. It's hard to know what she would've been thinking. There are some things we'll probably never know."

I tucked a wayward wave behind my ear. "Obviously, Pandora didn't have a clue Donna had really murdered Jenna. She lured Tim to her house, lying to him that she'd found evidence about what had happened to Jenna. That way, she could guarantee he'd turn up, and she could carry out her plan."

"We can't prove Pandora did it herself," Lester said skeptically.

"And can you prove that she didn't?' Vernon asked. "Tim Baxtor isn't a killer. If this goes to a trial, Tim's lawyer will be using our scenario to give the jurors reasonable doubt."

"And if you compare Pandora's fingerprints with ones found at the Danger Cove Vet Clinic, where the pentobarbital was stolen from, I bet you'll find a match. You were probably right about Donna sending me those threatening notes, because she knew we were digging into Jenna's disappearance too, and she wanted it to point toward Ian or someone else being involved to cover her tracks."

Lester stared into space for a while, hand resting in his chin. Then he stamped his foot under the table. "I'll need to compare those prints and then confer with the prosecutor and see what he has to say on the matter." He shook his head. "Damn. I was hoping for two arrests on my record. A Bonnie and Clyde special! Now I might have to make do with one?"

Vernon shook his head at him and stood up.

I slid my chair back and walked toward the door behind Vernon.

"Hey, Miss Marple and Columbo," Lester called out.

We turned back to him.

"Stay out of police business in the future." He wagged a chunky finger at us.

I opened the door and strolled out, muttering, "A thank-you would be nice."

Vernon grunted something under his breath.

We'd just reached the steps outside when we spotted Detective Bud Ohlsen coming toward us.

"Morning, Hope. Vernon."

"Morning."

"Sounds like you've had quite a busy week."

"You could say that."

He rocked back on his heels and looked at me. "I wanted to thank you for finding Jenna. It wasn't the ending I was hoping for, but it was an ending nevertheless."

I nodded up at him, then let him know what we thought about Pandora's death.

He stared up at the clouds, watching the wind drift them slowly over our heads, silent for a few moments as he took it all in. Then he looked back at me and sighed. "I think you're right. None of it really made sense to me. But now it clicks into place. If we find Pandora's prints at the vet's, then that'll pretty much prove your theory." He patted my arm. "Take care, both of you."

"You too."

CHAPTER TWENTY-SIX

———

Early the next morning I took a slow cycle ride around Danger Cove, savoring the wind in my hair and the sea air filtering into my lungs as I tried to shake off all the bad things that happened in the last week. Renewed and refreshed, I headed back for home, happy in the knowledge that things could get back to normal now. I parked my bike at the back of the building and walked around the side.

I was just unlocking the door, when Vernon appeared behind me. His cheeks had a healthier glow than I'd seen for months, and he had more of a bounce in his step, despite his limp.

"Morning! You're early," I said. "How're you feeling? You look a lot better, actually. Ruby's home cooking and natural remedies must be working wonders." I opened the door, and he followed me inside.

"Pah!" He waved a hand in the air. "She's got me eating tempeh and some weird stuff I can't even pronounce. And seaweed!" He shot me an incredulous look. "And beans, but not even nice baked beans that I used to slather over fried bacon. These ones are dressed in olive oil and herbs, or in casseroles, or in bean burgers! I don't know how much more my bowels can take. It's like living with the Taliban, taking orders from Ruby."

I smirked at his overdramatic protestations. "You love it! Admit it. And now you're both living under the same roof again..." I trailed off, letting that hang in the air for a while. "Maybe you should work on getting back together again. It's obvious you still love each other. And you shouldn't leave it until too late." I thought about my conversation with Ian. "One day you might wake up and find she's not here anymore."

He leaned his elbows on the bar. "I found out something interesting from my Seattle contact."

"Are you changing the subject, by any chance?" I swiped him with a dishcloth.

He grabbed the cloth from my hands in a lightning move and ignored the question. "Do you want to hear it?"

"Go on, then." I perched on the edge of a barstool.

"The fingerprints from the Danger Cove Vet Clinic matched Pandora's."

"So my theory was right. She took her own life and tried to frame Tim?"

"Uh-huh. Tim's been released, and Donna's arraignment hearing is today."

"I feel so sorry for Tim. But at least he's finally cleared his name."

"He's in shock at the moment, not surprisingly. He hadn't suspected Donna of killing Jenna in all these years. Now the poor guy has to pick up the pieces of his life yet again." He was just about to say something more, when Harvey walked in.

He stood in the entrance, a bouquet of forget-me-nots in his hands, that sexy smile on his face.

"I'm guessing they're still not for me?" Vernon nodded to the flowers.

"Er...unfortunately not, but I can get you some later." Harvey grinned, bringing out the laughter lines around his eyes. "How about some orange carnations? They'll bring out the color of your eyes."

Vernon laughed. "Well, I'll leave you lovebirds to it." He winked at me and disappeared into the kitchen to give us some privacy.

"Hey! They're gorgeous." I rounded the bar, walking toward him.

He glanced down at the flowers, then back to me. "These are an apology."

"For what?" My stomach sank to my knees. Was he going to tell me he'd slept with Carmen that night she was banging on his door in the early hours of the morning?

"For everything Carmen did to you and Karma."

"You can't apologize for her. And she didn't actually do anything to me. Just my poor cat."

"I know. She's completely bonkers. I had to pick her up from the hospital because she didn't have anyone else to help her. Luckily, at the moment she's on a plane back to the UK, crutches and all. But she did actually want me to apologize to you for what she tried to do to Karma, and for sending you those threatening notes. She realized she went too far."

"That was her?!"

"Yep."

"Wow. Well, I guess that clears that up. But at least we can start getting back to normal around here now. Can't we?" I looked up at him.

"I hope so." He handed the flowers over. "Anyway, these are *my* apology. Nothing to do with Carmen."

"For what?"

"I'm getting to that part. Do you know the story of these flowers?" he asked.

"Yes." I smiled. "But why don't you tell me anyway."

He took one of my hands in his free hand. "Well, legend has it that in medieval times a young knight was walking along the banks of a river with his girlfriend, and he bent down to pick them for her. But the weight of his armor caused him to fall into the river. As he was drowning, he threw the flowers to her on the bank and shouted out, 'Forget me not!'" He flashed me that dimple again. "Kind of depressing, actually, but...well, I wanted to say, er...sorry for neglecting you lately. And...um...er, you're always on...well, on my mind. And I'm not the kind of...um...guy who's, you know, unfaithful, and, well, please don't ever doubt my...er...feelings for... Oh God, I'm making a right mess of this, aren't I?"

I slid my hands around his neck, pulling him closer. So close I could feel his warm breath on my cheek, smell the outdoors on his skin. His nervousness was endearing, only making me love him more. "Not at all."

"Okay, so shall I go on?"

"Absolutely."

"Well, it's just that...I chose these flowers because even though I've neglected you lately with work...um...I could never forget you. You're one in a million, Hope, and—"

I kissed his neck tenderly.

"You're totally putting me off now." He slid his hand around my waist, his lips finding mine.

"So, you were saying?" I drew back, giving him a coy smile, a rush of longing hitting me.

He tossed the flowers on the bar, picked me up, and carried me up the stairs to my apartment. "I think you know what I'm saying," he said huskily, eyes hooded with a desire that matched mine.

"I think I do."

ABOUT THE AUTHORS

Sibel Hodge is the author of bestselling romantic comedy *Fourteen Days Later*. She has eight cats and one husband. In her spare time, she's Wonder Woman! When she's not out saving the world from dastardly demons, she writes books for adults and children.

Her work has been shortlisted for the Harry Bowling Prize 2008, Highly Commended by the Yeovil Literary Prize 2009, Runner-up in the Chapter One Promotions Novel Comp 2009, and nominated for Best Novel with Romantic Elements in 2010 by The Romance Reviews. Her novella *Trafficked: The Diary of a Sex Slave* has been listed as one of the Top 40 Books About Human Rights by Accredited Online Colleges.

To learn more about Sibel, visit her online at:
www.sibelhodge.com

Elizabeth Ashby was born and raised in Danger Cove and now uses her literary talent to tell stories about the town she knows and loves. Ms. Ashby has penned several Danger Cove Mysteries, which are published by Gemma Halliday Publishing. While she does admit to taking some poetic license in her storytelling, she loves to incorporate the real people and places of her hometown into her stories. She says anyone who visits Danger Cove is fair game for her poisoned pen, so tourists beware! When she's not writing, Ms. Ashby enjoys gardening, taking long walks along the Pacific coastline, and curling up with a hot cup of tea, her cat, Sherlock, and a thrilling novel.

Visit the official

DANGER COVE 🗡

website!

We're a sleepy little town in the Pacific Northwest and home to renowned mystery novelist, Elizabeth Ashby. Don't let out name fool you—we are the friendliest (if deadliest) small town you'll ever visit!

Meet the local residents, explore our interactive town map, and read about the next Danger Cove mystery!

www.dangercovemysteries.com

If you enjoyed *Killer Colada*, be sure to pick up these other Danger Cove Mysteries!

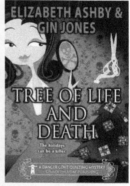

www.GemmaHallidayPublishing.com

CPSIA information can be obtained
at www.ICGtesting.com
Printed in the USA
LVHW052355220723
753203LV00009BA/215

9 781523 321131